Henry Kuttner

The Collected Works of Henry Kuttner

e-artnow 2020

Henry Kuttner

The Collected Works of Henry Kuttner

The Ego Machine, Where the World is Quiet, I, the Vampire, The Salem Horror, Chameleon Man

e-artnow, 2020
Contact: info@e-artnow.org

ISBN 978-80-273-0967-2

Contents

The Ego Machine

When a slightly mad robot drunk on AC, wants you to join an experiment in optimum ecology-don't do it! After all, who wants to argue like Disraeli or live like Ivan the Terrible?

CHAPTER I

Nicholas Martin looked up at the robot across the desk.

"I'm not going to ask what you want," he said, in a low, restrained voice. "I already know. Just go away and tell St. Cyr I approve. Tell him I think it's wonderful, putting a robot in the picture. We've had everything else by now, except the Rockettes. But clearly a quiet little play about Christmas among the Portuguese fishermen on the Florida coast *must* have a robot. Only, why not six robots? Tell him I suggest a baker's dozen. Go away."

"Was your mother's name Helena Glinska?" the robot asked.

"It was not," Martin said.

"Ah, then she must have been the Great Hairy One," the robot murmured.

Martin took his feet off the desk and sat up slowly.

"It's quite all right," the robot said hastily. "You've been chosen for an ecological experiment, that's all. But it won't hurt. Robots are perfectly normal life forms where I come from, so you needn't —"

"Shut up," Martin said. "Robot indeed, you-you bit-player! This time St. Cyr has gone too far." He began to shake slightly all over, with some repressed but strong emotion. The intercom box on the desk caught his eye, and he stabbed a finger at one of the switches. "Get me Miss Ashby! Right away!"

"I'm so sorry," the robot said apologetically. "Have I made a mistake? The threshold fluctuations in the neurons always upset my mnemonic norm when I temporalize. Isn't this a crisis-point in your life?"

Martin breathed hard, which seemed to confirm the robot's assumption.

"Exactly," it said. "The ecological imbalance approaches a peak that may destroy the life-form, unless ... mm-m. Now either you're about to be stepped on by a mammoth, locked in an iron mask, assassinated by helots, or-is this Sanskrit I'm speaking?" He shook his gleaming head. "Perhaps I should have got off fifty years ago, but I thought-sorry. Good-bye," he added hastily as Martin raised an angry glare.

Then the robot lifted a finger to each corner of his naturally rigid mouth, and moved his fingers horizontally in opposite directions, as though sketching an apologetic smile.

"No, don't go away," Martin said. "I want you right here, where the sight of you can refuel my rage in case it's needed. I wish to God I could get mad and stay mad," he added plaintively, gazing at the telephone.

"Are you sure your mother's name wasn't Helena Glinska?" the robot asked. It pinched thumb and forefinger together between its nominal brows, somehow giving the impression of a worried frown.

"Naturally I'm sure," Martin snapped.

"You aren't married yet, then? To Anastasia Zakharina-Koshkina?"

"Not yet or ever," Martin replied succinctly. The telephone rang. He snatched it up.

* * * * *

"Hello, Nick," said Erika Ashby's calm voice. "Something wrong?"

Instantly the fires of rage went out of Martin's eyes, to be replaced by a tender, rose-pink glow. For some years now he had given Erika, his very competent agent, ten percent of his take. He had also longed hopelessly to give her approximately a pound of flesh-the cardiac muscle, to put it in cold, unromantic terms. Martin did not; he put it in no terms at all, since whenever he tried to propose marriage to Erika he was taken with such fits of modesty that he could only babble o' green fields.

"Well," Erika repeated. "Something wrong?"

"Yes," Martin said, drawing a long breath. "Can St. Cyr make me marry somebody named Anastasia Zakharina-Koshkina?"

"What a wonderful memory you have," the robot put in mournfully. "Mine used to be, before I started temporalizing. But even radioactive neurons won't stand —"

"Nominally you're still entitled to life, liberty, et cetera," Erika said. "But I'm busy right now, Nick. Can't it wait till I see you?"

"When?"

"Didn't you get my message?" Erika demanded.

"Of course not," Martin said, angrily. "I've suspected for some time that all my incoming calls have to be cleared by St. Cyr. Somebody might try to smuggle in a word of hope, or possibly a file." His voice brightened. "Planning a jailbreak?"

"Oh, this is outrageous," Erika said. "Some day St. Cyr's going to go too far —"

"Not while he's got DeeDee behind him," Martin said gloomily. Summit Studios would sooner have made a film promoting atheism than offend their top box-office star, DeeDee Fleming. Even Tolliver Watt, who owned Summit lock, stock and barrel, spent wakeful nights because St. Cyr refused to let the lovely DeeDee sign a long-term contract.

"Nevertheless, Watt's no fool," Erika said. "I still think we could get him to give you a contract release if we could make him realize what a rotten investment you are. There isn't much time, though."

"Why not?"

"I told you-oh. Of course you don't know. He's leaving for Paris tomorrow morning."

Martin moaned. "Then I'm doomed," he said. "They'll pick up my option automatically next week and I'll never draw a free breath again. Erika, do something!"

"I'm going to," Erika said. "That's exactly what I want to see you about. Ah," she added suddenly, "now I understand why St. Cyr stopped my message. He was afraid. Nick, do you know what we've got to do?"

"See Watt?" Nick hazarded unhappily. "But Erika —"

"See Watt *alone*," Erika amplified.

"Not if St. Cyr can help it," Nick reminded her.

"Exactly. Naturally St. Cyr doesn't want us to talk to Watt privately. We might make him see reason. But this time, Nick, we've simply got to manage it somehow. One of us is going to talk to Watt while the other keeps St. Cyr at bay. Which do you choose?"

"Neither," Martin said promptly.

"Oh, Nick! I can't do the whole thing alone. Anybody'd think you were afraid of St. Cyr."

"I *am* afraid of St. Cyr," Martin said.

"Nonsense. What could he actually do to you?"

"He could terrorize me. He does it all the time. Erika, he says I'm indoctrinating beautifully. Doesn't it make your blood run cold? Look at all the other writers he's indoctrinated."

"I know. I saw one of them on Main Street last week, delving into garbage cans. Do you want to end up that way? Then stand up for your rights!"

"Ah," said the robot wisely, nodding. "Just as I thought. A crisis-point."

"Shut up," Martin said. "No, not you, Erika. I'm sorry."

"So am I," Erika said tartly. "For a moment I thought you'd acquired a backbone."

"If I were somebody like Hemingway —" Martin began in a miserable voice.

"Did you say Hemingway?" the robot inquired. "Is this the Kinsey-Hemingway era? Then I must be right. You're Nicholas Martin, the next subject. Martin, Martin? Let me see-oh yes, the Disraeli type, that's it." He rubbed his forehead with a grating sound. "Oh, my poor neuron thresholds! Now I remember."

* * * * *

"Nick, can you hear me?" Erika's voice inquired. "I'm coming over there right away. Brace yourself. We're going to beard St. Cyr in his den and convince Watt you'll never make a good screen-writer. Now —"

"But St. Cyr won't *ever* admit that," Martin cried. "He doesn't know the meaning of the word failure. He says so. He's going to make me into a screen-writer or kill me."

"Remember what happened to Ed Cassidy?" Erika reminded him grimly. "St. Cyr didn't make him into a screen-writer."

"True. Poor old Ed," Martin said, with a shiver.

"All right, then. I'm on my way. Anything else?"

"Yes!" Martin cried, drawing a deep breath. "Yes, there is! I love you madly!"

But the words never got past his glottis. Opening and closing his mouth noiselessly, the cowardly playwright finally clenched his teeth and tried again. A faint, hopeless squeak vibrated the telephone's disk. Martin let his shoulders slump hopelessly. It was clear he could never propose to anybody, not even a harmless telephone.

"Did you say something?" Erika asked. "Well, good-bye then."

"Wait a minute," Martin said, his eyes suddenly falling once more upon the robot. Speechless on one subject only, he went on rapidly, "I forgot to tell you. Watt and the nest-fouling St. Cyr have just hired a mock-up phony robot to play in *Angelina Noel!*"

But the line was dead.

"I'm not a phony," the robot said, hurt.

Martin fell back in his chair and stared at his guest with dull, hopeless eyes. "Neither was King Kong," he remarked. "Don't start feeding me some line St. Cyr's told you to pull. I know he's trying to break my nerve. He'll probably do it, too. Look what he's done to my play already. Why Fred Waring? I don't mind Fred Waring in his proper place. There he's fine. But not in *Angelina Noel.* Not as the Portuguese captain of a fishing boat manned by his entire band, accompanied by Dan Dailey singing *Napoli* to DeeDee Fleming in a mermaid's tail —"

Self-stunned by this recapitulation, Martin put his arms on the desk, his head in his hands, and to his horror found himself giggling. The telephone rang. Martin groped for the instrument without rising from his semi-recumbent position.

"Who?" he asked shakily. "Who? St. Cyr —"

A hoarse bellow came over the wire. Martin sat bolt upright, seizing the phone desperately with both hands.

"Listen!" he cried. "Will you let me finish what I'm going to say, just for once? Putting a robot in *Angelina Noel* is simply —"

"I do not hear what you say," roared a heavy voice. "Your idea stinks. Whatever it is. Be at Theater One for yesterday's rushes! At once!"

"But wait —"

St. Cyr belched and hung up. Martin's strangling hands tightened briefly on the telephone. But it was no use. The real strangle-hold was the one St. Cyr had around Martin's throat, and it had been tightening now for nearly thirteen weeks. Or had it been thirteen years? Looking backward, Martin could scarcely believe that only a short time ago he had been a free man, a successful Broadway playwright, the author of the hit play *Angelina Noel.* Then had come St. Cyr....

A snob at heart, the director loved getting his clutches on hit plays and name writers. Summit Studios, he had roared at Martin, would follow the original play exactly and would give Martin the final okay on the script, provided he signed a thirteen-week contract to help write the screen treatment. This had seemed too good to be true-and was.

Martin's downfall lay partly in the fine print and partly in the fact that Erika Ashby had been in the hospital with a bad attack of influenza at the time. Buried in legal verbiage was a clause that bound Martin to five years of servitude with Summit should they pick up his option. Next week they would certainly do just that, unless justice prevailed.

* * * * *

"I think I need a drink," Martin said unsteadily. "Or several." He glanced toward the robot. "I wonder if you'd mind getting me that bottle of Scotch from the bar over there."

"But I am here to conduct an experiment in optimum ecology," said the robot.

Martin closed his eyes. "Pour me a drink," he pleaded. "Please. Then put the glass in my hand, will you? It's not much to ask. After all, we're both human beings, aren't we?"

"Well, no," the robot said, placing a brimming glass in Martin's groping fingers. Martin drank. Then he opened his eyes and blinked at the tall highball glass in his hand. The robot had filled it to the brim with Scotch. Martin turned a wondering gaze on his metallic companion.

"You must do a lot of drinking yourself," he said thoughtfully. "I suppose tolerance can be built up. Go ahead. Help yourself. Take the rest of the bottle."

The robot placed the tip of a finger above each eye and slid the fingers upward, as though raising his eyebrows inquiringly.

"Go on, have a jolt," Martin urged. "Or don't you want to break bread with me, under the circumstances?"

"How can I?" the robot asked. "I'm a robot." His voice sounded somewhat wistful. "What happens?" he inquired. "Is it a lubricatory or a fueling mechanism?"

Martin glanced at his brimming glass.

"Fueling," he said tersely. "High octane. You really believe in staying in character, don't you? Why not —"

"Oh, the principle of irritation," the robot interrupted. "I see. Just like fermented mammoth's milk."

Martin choked. "Have you ever drunk fermented mammoth's milk?" he inquired.

"How could I?" the robot asked. "But I've seen it done." He drew a straight line vertically upward between his invisible eyebrows, managing to look wistful. "Of course my world is perfectly functional and functionally perfect, but I can't help finding temporalizing a fascina —" He broke off. "I'm wasting space-time. Ah. Now. Mr. Martin, would you be willing to —"

"Oh, have a drink," Martin said. "I feel hospitable. Go ahead, indulge me, will you? My pleasures are few. And I've got to go and be terrorized in a minute, anyhow. If you can't get that mask off I'll send for a straw. You can step out of character long enough for one jolt, can't you?"

"I'd like to try it," the robot said pensively. "Ever since I noticed the effect fermented mammoth's milk had on the boys, it's been on my mind, rather. Quite easy for a human, of course. Technically it's simple enough, I see now. The irritation just increases the frequency of the brain's kappa waves, as with boosted voltage, but since electrical voltage never existed in pre-robot times —"

"It did," Martin said, taking another drink. "I mean, it does. What do you call that, a mammoth?" He indicated the desk lamp.

The robot's jaw dropped.

"That?" he asked in blank amazement. "Why-why then all those telephone poles and dynamos and lighting-equipment I noticed in this era are powered by electricity!"

"What did you think they were powered by?" Martin asked coldly.

"Slaves," the robot said, examining the lamp. He switched it on, blinked, and then unscrewed the bulb. "Voltage, you say?"

"Don't be a fool," Martin said. "You're overplaying your part. I've got to get going in a minute. Do you want a jolt or don't you?"

"Well," the robot said, "I don't want to seem unsociable. This *ought* to work." So saying, he stuck his finger in the lamp-socket. There was a brief, crackling flash. The robot withdrew his finger.

"*F(t)* —" he said, and swayed slightly. Then his fingers came up and sketched a smile that seemed, somehow, to express delighted surprise.

"*Fff(t)!*" he said, and went on rather thickly, "*F(t)* integral between plus and minus infinity ... *a-sub-n* to *e*...."

Martin's eyes opened wide with shocked horror. Whether a doctor or a psychiatrist should be called in was debatable, but it was perfectly evident that this was a case for the medical profession, and the sooner the better. Perhaps the police, too. The bit-player in the robot suit was clearly as mad as a hatter. Martin poised indecisively, waiting for his lunatic guest either to drop dead or spring at his throat.

The robot appeared to be smacking his lips, with faint clicking sounds.

"Why, that's wonderful," he said. "AC, too."

"Y-you're not dead?" Martin inquired shakily.

"I'm not even alive," the robot murmured. "The way you'd understand it, that is. Ah-thanks for the jolt."

* * * * *

Martin stared at the robot with the wildest dawning of surmise.

"Why —" he gasped. "Why —*you're a robot!*"

"Certainly I'm a robot," his guest said. "What slow minds you pre-robots had. Mine's working like lightning now." He stole a drunkard's glance at the desk-lamp. "*F(t)* —I mean, if you counted the kappa waves of my radio-atomic brain now, you'd be amazed how the frequency's increased." He paused thoughtfully. "*F(t)*," he added.

Moving quite slowly, like a man under water, Martin lifted his glass and drank whiskey. Then, cautiously, he looked up at the robot again.

"*F(t)* —" he said, paused, shuddered, and drank again. That did it. "I'm drunk," he said with an air of shaken relief. "That must be it. I was almost beginning to believe —"

"Oh, nobody believes I'm a robot at first," the robot said. "You'll notice I showed up in a movie lot, where I wouldn't arouse suspicion. I'll appear to Ivan Vasilovich in an alchemist's lab, and he'll jump to the conclusive I'm an automaton. Which, of course, I *am*. Then there's a Uighur on my list —I'll appear to him in a shaman's hut and he'll assume I'm a devil. A matter of ecologicologic."

"Then you're a devil?" Martin inquired, seizing on the only plausible solution.

"No, no, no. I'm a robot. Don't you understand anything?"

"I don't even know who I am, now," Martin said. "For all I know, I'm a faun and you're a human child. I don't think this Scotch is doing me as much good as I'd —"

"Your name is Nicholas Martin," the robot said patiently. "And mine is Eniac."

"Eniac?"

"Eniac," the robot corrected, capitalizing. "Eniac Gamma the Ninety-Third."

So saying, he unslung a sack from his metallic shoulder and began to rummage out length upon length of what looked like red silk ribbon with a curious metallic lustre. After approximately a quarter-mile of it had appeared, a crystal football helmet emerged attached to its end. A gleaming red-green stone was set on each side of the helmet.

"Just over the temporal lobes, you see," the robot explained, indicating the jewels. "Now you just set it on your head, like this —"

"Oh no I don't," Martin said, withdrawing his head with the utmost rapidity. "Neither do you, my friend. What's the idea? I don't like the looks of that gimmick. I particularly don't like those two red garnets on the sides. They look like eyes."

"Those are artificial eclogite," the robot assured him. "They simply have a high dielectric constant. It's merely a matter of altering the normal thresholds of the neuron memory-circuits. All thinking is based on memory, you know. The strength of your associations-the emotional indices of your memories-channel your actions and decisions, and the ecologizer simply changes the voltage of your brain so the thresholds are altered."

"Is that all it does?" Martin asked suspiciously.

"Well, now," the robot said with a slight air of evasion. "I didn't intend to mention it, but since you ask-it also imposes the master-matrix of your character type. But since that's the prototype of your character in the first place, it will simply enable you to make the most of your potential ability, hereditary and acquired. It will make you react to your environment in the way that best assures your survival."

"Not me, it won't," Martin said firmly. "Because you aren't going to put that thing on my head."

The robot sketched a puzzled frown. "Oh," he said after a pause. "I haven't explained yet, have I? It's very simple. Would you be willing to take part in a valuable socio-cultural experiment for the benefit of all mankind?"

"No," Martin said.

"But you don't know what it is yet," the robot said plaintively. "You'll be the only one to refuse, after I've explained everything thoroughly. By the way, can you understand me all right?"

Martin laughed hollowly. "Natch," he said.

"Good," the robot said, relieved. "That may be one trouble with my memory. I had to record so many languages before I could temporalize. Sanskrit's very simple, but medieval Russian's confusing, and as for Uighur-however! The purpose of this experiment is to promote the most successful pro-survival relationship between man and his environment. Instant adaptation is what we're aiming at, and we hope to get it by minimizing the differential between individual and environment. In other words, the right reaction at the right time. Understand?"

"Of course not," Martin said. "What nonsense you talk."

"There are," the robot said rather wearily, "only a limited number of character matrices possible, depending first on the arrangement of the genes within the chromosomes, and later upon environmental additions. Since environments tend to repeat-like societies, you know-an organizational pattern isn't hard to lay out, along the Kaldekooz time-scale. You follow me so far?"

"By the Kaldekooz time-scale, yes," Martin said.

"I was always lucid," the robot remarked a little vainly, nourishing a swirl of red ribbon.

"Keep that thing away from me," Martin complained. "Drunk I may be, but I have no intention of sticking my neck out that far."

"Of course you'll do it," the robot said firmly. "Nobody's ever refused yet. And don't bicker with me or you'll get me confused and I'll have to take another jolt of voltage. Then there's no telling how confused I'll be. My memory gives me enough trouble when I temporalize. Time-travel always raises the synaptic delay threshold, but the trouble is it's so variable. That's why I got you mixed up with Ivan at first. But I don't visit him till after I've seen you —I'm running the test chronologically, and nineteen-fifty-two comes before fifteen-seventy, of course."

"It doesn't," Martin said, tilting the glass to his lips. "Not even in Hollywood does nineteen-fifty-two come before fifteen-seventy."

"I'm using the Kaldekooz time-scale," the robot explained. "But really only for convenience. Now do you want the ideal ecological differential or don't you? Because —" Here he flourished the red ribbon again, peered into the helmet, looked narrowly at Martin, and shook his head.

"I'm sorry," the robot said. "I'm afraid this won't work. Your head's too small. Not enough brain-room, I suppose. This helmet's for an eight and a half head, and yours is much too —"

"My head is eight and a half," Martin protested with dignity.

"Can't be," the robot said cunningly. "If it were, the helmet would fit, and it doesn't. Too big."

"It does fit," Martin said.

"That's the trouble with arguing with pre-robot species," Eniac said, as to himself. "Low, brutish, unreasoning. No wonder, when their heads are so small. Now Mr. Martin —" He spoke as though to a small, stupid, stubborn child. "Try to understand. This helmet's size eight and a half. Your head is unfortunately so very small that the helmet wouldn't fit —"

"Blast it!" cried the infuriated Martin, caution quite lost between Scotch and annoyance. "It does fit! Look here!" Recklessly he snatched the helmet and clapped it firmly on his head. "It fits perfectly!"

"I erred," the robot acknowledged, with such a gleam in his eye that Martin, suddenly conscious of his rashness, jerked the helmet from his head and dropped it on the desk. Eniac quietly picked it up and put it back into his sack, stuffing the red ribbon in after it with rapid motions. Martin watched, baffled, until Eniac had finished, gathered together the mouth of the sack, swung it on his shoulder again, and turned toward the door.

"Good-bye," the robot said. "And thank you."

"For what?" Martin demanded.

"For your cooperation," the robot said.

"I won't cooperate," Martin told him flatly. "It's no use. Whatever fool treatment it is you're selling, I'm not going to —"

"Oh, you've already had the ecology treatment," Eniac replied blandly. "I'll be back tonight to renew the charge. It lasts only twelve hours."

"*What!*"

Eniac moved his forefingers outward from the corners of his mouth, sketching a polite smile. Then he stepped through the door and closed it behind him.

Martin made a faint squealing sound, like a stuck but gagged pig.

Something was happening inside his head.

Nicholas Martin felt like a man suddenly thrust under an ice-cold shower. No, not cold-steaming hot. Perfumed, too. The wind that blew in from the open window bore with it a frightful stench of gasoline, sagebrush, paint, and-from the distant commissary-ham sandwiches.

"Drunk," he thought frantically. "I'm drunk-or crazy!" He sprang up and spun around wildly; then catching sight of a crack in the hardwood floor he tried to walk along it. "Because if I can walk a straight line," he thought, "I'm not drunk. I'm only crazy...." It was not a very comforting thought.

He could walk it, all right. He could walk a far straighter line than the crack, which he saw now was microscopically jagged. He had, in fact, never felt such a sense of location and equilibrium in his life. His experiment carried him across the room to a wall-mirror, and as he straightened to look into it, suddenly all confusion settled and ceased. The violent sensory perceptions leveled off and returned to normal.

Everything was quiet. Everything was all right.

Martin met his own eyes in the mirror.

Everything was *not* all right.

He was stone cold sober. The Scotch he had drunk might as well have been spring-water. He leaned closer to the mirror, trying to stare through his own eyes into the depths of his brain. For something extremely odd was happening in there. All over his brain, tiny shutters were beginning to move, some sliding up till only a narrow crack remained, through which the beady little eyes of neurons could be seen peeping, some sliding down with faint crashes, revealing the agile, spidery forms of still other neurons scuttling for cover.

Altered thresholds, changing the yes-and-no reaction time of the memory-circuits, with their key emotional indices and associations ... huh?

The robot!

Martin's head swung toward the closed office door. But he made no further move. The look of blank panic on his face very slowly, quite unconsciously, began to change. The robot ... could wait.

Automatically Martin raised his hand, as though to adjust an invisible monocle. Behind him, the telephone began to ring. Martin glanced at it.

His lips curved into an insolent smile.

Flicking dust from his lapel with a suave gesture, Martin picked up the telephone. He said nothing. There was a long silence. Then a hoarse voice shouted, "Hello, hello, hello! Are you there? You, Martin!"

Martin said absolutely nothing at all.

"You keep me waiting," the voice bellowed. "Me, St. Cyr! Now jump! The rushes are ... Martin, do you hear me?"

Martin gently laid down the receiver on the desk. He turned again toward the mirror, regarded himself critically, frowned.

"Dreary," he murmured. "Distinctly dreary. I wonder why I ever bought this necktie?"

The softly bellowing telephone distracted him. He studied the instrument briefly, then clapped his hands sharply together an inch from the mouthpiece. There was a sharp, anguished cry from the other end of the line.

"Very good," Martin murmured, turning away. "That robot has done me a considerable favor. I should have realized the possibilities sooner. After all, a super-machine, such as Eniac, would be far cleverer than a man, who is merely an ordinary machine. Yes," he added, stepping into the hall and coming face to face with Toni LaMotta, who was currently working for Summit on loan. "'*Man is a machine, and woman —*'" Here he gave Miss LaMotta a look of such arrogant significance that she was quite startled.

"'*And woman —a toy,*'" Martin amplified, as he turned toward Theater One, where St. Cyr and destiny awaited him.

Summit Studios, outdoing even MGM, always shot ten times as much footage as necessary on every scene. At the beginning of each shooting day, this confusing mass of celluloid was shown in St. Cyr's private projection theater, a small but luxurious domed room furnished with lie-back chairs and every other convenience, though no screen was visible until you looked up. Then you saw it on the ceiling.

When Martin entered, it was instantly evident that ecology took a sudden shift toward the worse. Operating on the theory that the old Nicholas Martin had come into it, the theater, which had breathed an expensive air of luxurious confidence, chilled toward him. The nap of the Persian rug shrank from his contaminating feet. The chair he stumbled against in the half-light seemed to shrug contemptuously. And the three people in the theater gave him such a look as might be turned upon one of the larger apes who had, by sheer accident, got an invitation to Buckingham Palace.

DeeDee Fleming (her real name was impossible to remember, besides having not a vowel in it) lay placidly in her chair, her feet comfortably up, her lovely hands folded, her large, liquid gaze fixed upon the screen where DeeDee Fleming, in the silvery meshes of a technicolor mermaid, swam phlegmatically through seas of pearl-colored mist.

Martin groped in the gloom for a chair. The strangest things were going on inside his brain, where tiny stiles still moved and readjusted until he no longer felt in the least like Nicholas Martin. Who did he feel like, then? What had happened?

He recalled the neurons whose beady little eyes he had fancied he saw staring brightly into, as well as out of, his own. Or had he? The memory was vivid, yet it couldn't be, of course. The answer was perfectly simple and terribly logical. Eniac Gamma the Ninety-Third had told him, somewhat ambiguously, just what his ecological experiment involved. Martin had merely been given the optimum reactive pattern of his successful prototype, a man who had most thoroughly controlled his own environment. And Eniac had told him the man's name, along with several confusing references to other prototypes like an Ivan (who?) and an unnamed Uighur.

The name for Martin's prototype was, of course, Disraeli, Earl of Beaconsfield. Martin had a vivid recollection of George Arliss playing the role. Clever, insolent, eccentric in dress and manner, exuberant, suave, self-controlled, with a strongly perceptive imagination....

"No, no, no!" DeeDee said with a sort of calm impatience. "Be careful, Nick. Some other chair, please. I have my feet on this one."

"T-t-t-t-t," said Raoul St. Cyr, protruding his thick lips and snapping the fingers of an enormous hand as he pointed to a lowly chair against the wall. "Behind me, Martin. Sit down, sit down. Out of our way. Now! Pay attention. Study what I have done to make something great out of your foolish little play. Especially note how I have so cleverly ended the solo by building to five cumulative pratt-falls. Timing is all," he finished. "Now-Silence!"

For a man born in the obscure little Balkan country of Mixo-Lydia, Raoul St. Cyr had done very well for himself in Hollywood. In 1939 St. Cyr, growing alarmed at the imminence of war, departed for America, taking with him the print of an unpronounceable Mixo-Lydian film he had made, which might be translated roughly as *The Pores In the Face of the Peasant*.

With this he established his artistic reputation as a great director, though if the truth were known, it was really poverty that caused *The Pores* to be so artistically lighted, and simple drunkenness which had made most of the cast act out one of the strangest performances in film history. But critics compared *The Pores* to a ballet and praised inordinately the beauty of its leading lady, now known to the world as DeeDee Fleming.

DeeDee was so incredibly beautiful that the law of compensation would force one to expect incredible stupidity as well. One was not disappointed. DeeDee's neurons didn't know *anything*. She had heard of emotions, and under St. Cyr's bullying could imitate a few of them, but other directors had gone mad trying to get through the semantic block that kept DeeDee's mind a calm, unruffled pool possibly three inches deep. St. Cyr merely bellowed. This simple, primordial approach seemed to be the only one that made sense to Summit's greatest investment and top star.

With this whip-hand over the beautiful and brainless DeeDee, St. Cyr quickly rose to the top in Hollywood. He had undoubted talent. He could make one picture very well indeed. He had made it twenty times already, each time starring DeeDee, and each time perfecting his own feudalistic production unit. Whenever anyone disagreed with St. Cyr, he had only to threaten to go over to MGM and take the obedient DeeDee with him, for he had never allowed her to sign a long-term contract and she worked only on a picture-to-picture basis. Even Tolliver Watt knuckled under when St. Cyr voiced the threat of removing DeeDee.

* * * * *

"Sit down, Martin," Tolliver Watt said. He was a tall, lean, hatchet-faced man who looked like a horse being starved because he was too proud to eat hay. With calm, detached omnipotence he inclined his grey-shot head a millimeter, while a faintly pained expression passed fleetingly across his face.

"Highball, please," he said.

A white-clad waiter appeared noiselessly from nowhere and glided forward with a tray. It was at this point that Martin felt the last stiles readjust in his brain, and entirely on impulse he reached out and took the frosted highball glass from the tray. Without observing this the waiter glided on and presented Watt with a gleaming salver full of nothing. Watt and the waiter regarded the tray.

Then their eyes met. There was a brief silence.

"Here," Martin said, replacing the glass. "Much too weak. Get me another, please. I'm reorienting toward a new phase, which means a different optimum," he explained to the puzzled Watt as he readjusted a chair beside the great man and dropped into it. Odd that he had never before felt at ease during rushes. Right now he felt fine. Perfectly at ease. Relaxed.

"Scotch and soda for Mr. Martin," Watt said calmly. "And another for me."

"So, so, so, now we begin," St. Cyr cried impatiently. He spoke into a hand microphone. Instantly the screen on the ceiling flickered noisily and began to unfold a series of rather ragged scenes in which a chorus of mermaids danced on their tails down the street of a little Florida fishing village.

To understand the full loathsomeness of the fate facing Nicholas Martin, it is necessary to view a St. Cyr production. It seemed to Martin that he was watching the most noisome movie ever put upon film. He was conscious that St. Cyr and Watt were stealing rather mystified glances at him. In the dark he put up two fingers and sketched a robot-like grin. Then, feeling sublimely sure of himself, he lit a cigarette and chuckled aloud.

"You laugh?" St. Cyr demanded with instant displeasure. "You do not appreciate great art? What do you know about it, eh? Are you a genius?"

"This," Martin said urbanely, "is the most noisome movie ever put on film."

In the sudden, deathly quiet which followed, Martin flicked ashes elegantly and added, "With my help, you may yet avoid becoming the laughing stock of the whole continent. Every foot of this picture must be junked. Tomorrow bright and early we will start all over, and —"

Watt said quietly, "We're quite competent to make a film out of *Angelina Noel*, Martin."

"It is artistic!" St. Cyr shouted. "And it will make money, too!"

"Bah, money!" Martin said cunningly. He flicked more ash with a lavish gesture. "Who cares about money? Let Summit worry."

Watt leaned forward to peer searchingly at Martin in the dimness.

"Raoul," he said, glancing at St. Cyr, "I understood you were getting your-ah-your new writers whipped into shape. This doesn't sound to me as if —"

"Yes, yes, yes, yes," St. Cyr cried excitedly. "Whipped into shape, exactly! A brief delirium, eh? Martin, you feel well? You feel yourself?"

Martin laughed with quiet confidence. "Never fear," he said. "The money you spend on me is well worth what I'll bring you in prestige. I quite understand. Our confidential talks were not to be secret from Watt, of course."

"What confidential talks?" bellowed St. Cyr thickly, growing red.

"We need keep nothing from Watt, need we?" Martin went on imperturably. "You hired me for prestige, and prestige you'll get, if you can only keep your big mouth shut long enough. I'll make the name of St. Cyr glorious for you. Naturally you may lose something at the box-office, but it's well worth —"

"*Pjrzqxgl!*" roared St. Cyr in his native tongue, and he lumbered up from the chair, brandishing the microphone in an enormous, hairy hand.

Deftly Martin reached out and twitched it from his grasp.

"Stop the film," he ordered crisply.

It was very strange. A distant part of his mind knew that normally he would never have dared behave this way, but he felt convinced that never before in his life had he acted with complete normality. He glowed with a giddy warmth of confidence that everything he did would be right, at least while the twelve-hour treatment lasted....

* * * * *

The screen flickered hesitantly, then went blank.

"Turn the lights on," Martin ordered the unseen presence beyond the mike. Softly and suddenly the room glowed with illumination. And upon the visages of Watt and St. Cyr he saw a mutual dawning uneasiness begin to break.

He had just given them food for thought. But he had given them more than that. He tried to imagine what moved in the minds of the two men, below the suspicions he had just implanted. St. Cyr's was fairly obvious. The Mixo-Lydian licked his lips-no mean task-and studied Martin with uneasy little bloodshot eyes. Clearly Martin had acquired confidence from somewhere. What did it mean? What secret sin of St. Cyr's had been discovered to him, what flaw in his contract, that he dared behave so defiantly?

Tolliver Watt was a horse of another color; apparently the man had no guilty secrets; but he too looked uneasy. Martin studied the proud face and probed for inner weaknesses. Watt would be a harder nut to crack. But Martin could do it.

"That last underwater sequence," he now said, pursuing his theme. "Pure trash, you know. It'll have to come out. The whole scene must be shot from under water."

"Shut up!" St. Cyr shouted violently.

"But it must, you know," Martin went on. "Or it won't jibe with the new stuff I've written in. In fact, I'm not at all certain that the whole picture shouldn't be shot under water. You know, we could use the documentary technique —"

"Raoul," Watt said suddenly, "what's this man trying to do?"

"He is trying to break his contract, of course," St. Cyr said, turning ruddy olive. "It is the bad phase all my writers go through before I get them whipped into shape. In Mixo-Lydia —"

"Are you sure he'll whip into shape?" Watt asked.

"To me this is now a personal matter," St. Cyr said, glaring at Martin. "I have spent nearly thirteen weeks on this man and I do not intend to waste my valuable time on another. I tell you he is simply trying to break his contract-tricks, tricks, tricks."

"Are you?" Watt asked Martin coldly.

"Not now," Martin said. "I've changed my mind. My agent insists I'd be better off away from Summit. In fact, she has the curious feeling that I and Summit would suffer by a mesalliance. But for the first time I'm not sure I agree. I begin to see possibilities, even in the tripe St. Cyr has been stuffing down the public's throat for years. Of course I can't work miracles all at once. Audiences have come to expect garbage from Summit, and they've even been conditioned to like it. But we'll begin in a small way to re-educate them with this picture. I suggest we try to symbolize the Existentialist hopelessness of it all by ending the film with a full four hundred feet of seascapes-nothing but vast, heaving stretches of ocean," he ended, on a note of complacent satisfaction.

A vast, heaving stretch of Raoul St. Cyr rose from his chair and advanced upon Martin. "Outside, outside!" he shouted. "Back to your cell, you double-crossing vermin! I, Raoul St. Cyr, command it. Outside, before I rip you limb from limb —"

Martin spoke quickly. His voice was calm, but he knew he would have to work fast.

"You see, Watt?" he said clearly, meeting Watt's rather startled gaze. "Doesn't dare let you exchange three words with me, for fear I'll let something slip. No wonder he's trying to put me out of here-he's skating on thin ice these days."

Goaded, St. Cyr rolled forward in a ponderous lunge, but Watt interposed. It was true, of course, that the writer was probably trying to break his contract. But there were wheels within wheels here. Martin was too confident, too debonaire. Something was going on which Watt did not understand.

"All right, Raoul," he said decisively. "Relax for a minute. I said relax! We don't want Nick here suing you for assault and battery, do we? Your artistic temperament carries you away sometimes. Relax and let's hear what Nick has to say."

"Watch out for him, Tolliver!" St. Cyr cried warningly. "They're cunning, these creatures. Cunning as rats. You never know —"

Martin raised the microphone with a lordly gesture. Ignoring the director, he said commandingly into the mike, "Put me through to the commissary. The bar, please. Yes. I want to order a drink. Something very special. A —ah —a Helena Glinska —"

* * * * *

"Hello," Erika Ashby's voice said from the door. "Nick, are you there? May I come in?"

The sound of her voice sent delicious chills rushing up and down Martin's spine. He swung round, mike in hand, to welcome her. But St. Cyr, pleased at this diversion, roared before he could speak.

"No, no, no, no! Go! Go at once. Whoever you are —*out!*"

Erika, looking very brisk, attractive and firm, marched into the room and cast at Martin a look of resigned patience.

Very clearly she expected to fight both her own battles and his.

"I'm on business here," she told St. Cyr coldly. "You can't part author and agent like this. Nick and I want to have a word with Mr. Watt."

"Ah, my pretty creature, sit down," Martin said in a loud, clear voice, scrambling out of his chair. "Welcome! I'm just ordering myself a drink. Will you have something?"

Erika looked at him with startled suspicion. "No, and neither will you," she said. "How many have you had already? Nick, if you're drunk at a time like this —"

"And no shilly-shallying," Martin said blandly into the mike. "I want it at once, do you hear? A Helena Glinska, yes. Perhaps you don't know it? Then listen carefully. Take the largest Napoleon you've got. If you haven't a big one, a small punch bowl will do. Fill it half full with ice-cold ale. Got that? Add three jiggers of creme de menthe —"

"Nick, are you mad?" Erika demanded, revolted.

" —and six jiggers of honey," Martin went on placidly. "Stir, don't shake. Never shake a Helena Glinska. Keep it well chilled, and —"

"Miss Ashby, we are very busy," St. Cyr broke in importantly, making shooing motions toward the door. "Not now. Sorry. You interrupt. Go at once."

" —better add six more jiggers of honey," Martin was heard to add contemplatively into the mike. "And then send it over immediately. Drop everything else, and get it here within sixty seconds. There's a bonus for you if you do. Okay? Good. See to it."

He tossed the microphone casually at St. Cyr.

Meanwhile, Erika had closed in on Tolliver Watt.

"I've just come from talking to Gloria Eden," she said, "and she's willing to do a one-picture deal with Summit *if* I okay it. But I'm not going to okay it unless you release Nick Martin from his contract, and that's flat."

Watt showed pleased surprise.

"Well, we might get together on that," he said instantly, for he was a fan of Miss Eden's and for a long time had yearned to star her in a remake of *Vanity Fair*. "Why didn't you bring her along? We could have —"

"Nonsense!" St. Cyr shouted. "Do not discuss this matter yet, Tolliver."

"She's down at Laguna," Erika explained. "Be quiet, St. Cyr! I won't —"

A knock at the door interrupted her. Martin hurried to open it and as he had expected encountered a waiter with a tray.

"Quick work," he said urbanely, accepting the huge, coldly sweating Napoleon in a bank of ice. "Beautiful, isn't it?"

St. Cyr's booming shouts from behind him drowned out whatever remark the waiter may have made as he received a bill from Martin and withdrew, looking nauseated.

"No, no, no, no," St. Cyr was roaring. "Tolliver, we can get Gloria and keep this writer too, not that he is any good, but I have spent already thirteen weeks training him in the St. Cyr approach. Leave it to me. In Mixo-Lydia we handle —"

Erika's attractive mouth was opening and shutting, her voice unheard in the uproar. St. Cyr could keep it up indefinitely, as was well known in Hollywood. Martin sighed, lifted the brimming Napoleon and sniffed delicately as he stepped backward toward his chair. When his heel touched it, he tripped with the utmost grace and savoir-faire, and very deftly emptied the Helena Glinsak, ale, honey, creme de menthe, ice and all, over St. Cyr's capacious front.

St. Cyr's bellow broke the microphone.

* * * * *

Martin had composed his invention carefully. The nauseous brew combined the maximum elements of wetness, coldness, stickiness and pungency.

The drenched St. Cyr, shuddering violently as the icy beverage deluged his legs, snatched out his handkerchief and mopped in vain. The handkerchief merely stuck to his trousers, glued there by twelve jiggers of honey. He reeked of peppermint.

"I suggest we adjourn to the commissary," Martin said fastidiously. "In some private booth we can go on with this discussion away from the-the rather overpowering smell of peppermint."

"In Mixo-Lydia," St. Cyr gasped, sloshing in his shoes as he turned toward Martin, "in Mixo-Lydia we throw to the dogs-we boil in oil-we —"

"And next time," Martin said, "please don't joggle my elbow when I'm holding a Helena Glinska. It's most annoying."

St. Cyr drew a mighty breath, rose to his full height-and then subsided. St. Cyr at the moment looked like a Keystone Kop after the chase sequence, and knew it. Even if he killed Martin now, the element of classic tragedy would be lacking. He would appear in the untenable position of Hamlet murdering his uncle with custard pies.

"Do nothing until I return!" he commanded, and with a final glare at Martin plunged moistly out of the theater.

The door crashed shut behind him. There was silence for a moment except for the soft music from the overhead screen which DeeDee had caused to be turned on again, so that she might watch her own lovely form flicker in dimmed images through pastel waves, while she sang a duet with Dan Dailey about sailors, mermaids and her home in far Atlantis.

"And now," said Martin, turning with quiet authority to Watt, who was regarding him with a baffled expression, "I want a word with you."

"I can't discuss your contract till Raoul gets back," Watt said quickly.

"Nonsense," Martin said in a firm voice. "Why should St. Cyr dictate your decisions? Without you, he couldn't turn out a box-office success if he had to. No, be quiet, Erika. I'm handling this, my pretty creature."

Watt rose to his feet. "Sorry, I can't discuss it," he said. "St. Cyr pictures make money, and you're an inexperien —"

"That's why I see the true situation so clearly," Martin said. "The trouble with you is you draw a line between artistic genius and financial genius. To you, it's merely routine when you work with the plastic medium of human minds, shaping them into an Ideal Audience. You are an ecological genius, Tolliver Watt! The true artist controls his environment, and gradually you, with a master's consummate skill, shape that great mass of living, breathing humanity into a perfect audience...."

"Sorry," Watt said, but not, bruskly. "I really have no time-ah —"

"Your genius has gone long enough unrecognized," Martin said hastily, letting admiration ring in his golden voice. "You assume that St. Cyr is your equal. You give him your own credit titles. Yet in your own mind you must have known that half the credit for his pictures is yours. Was Phidias non-commercial? Was Michaelangelo? Commercialism is simply a label for functionalism, and all great artists produce functional art. The trivial details of Rubens' masterpieces were filled in by assistants, were they not? But Rubens got the credit, not his hirelings. The proof of the pudding's obvious. Why?" Cunningly gauging his listener, Martin here broke off.

"Why?" Watt asked.

"Sit down," Martin urged. "I'll tell you why. St. Cyr's pictures make money, but you're responsible for their molding into the ideal form, impressing your character-matrix upon everything and everyone at Summit Studios...."

* * * * *

Slowly Watt sank into his chair. About his ears the hypnotic bursts of Disraelian rhodomontade thundered compellingly. For Martin had the man hooked. With unerring aim he had at the first try discovered Watt's weakness-the uncomfortable feeling in a professionally arty town that money-making is a basically contemptible business. Disraeli had handled tougher problems in his day. He had swayed Parliaments.

Watt swayed, tottered-and fell. It took about ten minutes, all in all. By the end of that time, dizzy with eloquent praise of his economic ability, Watt had realized that while St. Cyr might be an artistic genius, he had no business interfering in the plans of an economic genius. Nobody told Watt what to do when economics were concerned.

"You have the broad vision that can balance all possibilities and show the right path with perfect clarity," Martin said glibly. "Very well. You wish Eden. You feel-do you not? —that I am unsuitable material. Only geniuses can change their plans with instantaneous speed.... When will my contract release be ready?"

"What?" said Watt, in a swimming, glorious daze. "Oh. Of course. Hm-m. Your contract release. Well, now —"

"St. Cyr would stubbornly cling to past errors until Summit goes broke," Martin pointed out. "Only a genius like Tolliver Watt strikes when the iron is hot, when he sees a chance to exchange failure for success, a Martin for an Eden."

"Hm-m," Watt said. "Yes. Very well, then." His long face grew shrewd. "Very, well, you get your release —*after* I've signed Eden."

"There you put your finger on the heart of the matter," Martin approved, after a very brief moment of somewhat dashed thought. "Miss Eden is still undecided. If you left the transaction to somebody like St. Cyr, say, it would be botched. Erika, you have your car here? How quickly could you drive Tolliver Watt to Laguna? He's the only person with the skill to handle this situation."

"What situa-oh, yes. Of course, Nick. We could start right away."

"But —" Watt said.

The Disraeli-matrix swept on into oratorical periods that made the walls ring. The golden tongue played arpeggios with logic.

"I see," the dazed Watt murmured, allowing himself to be shepherded toward the door. "Yes, yes, of course. Then-suppose you drop over to my place tonight, Martin. After I get the Eden signature, I'll have your release prepared. Hm-m. Functional genius...." His voice fell to a low, crooning mutter, and he moved quietly out of the door.

Martin laid a hand on Erika's arm as she followed him.

"Wait a second," he said. "Keep him away from the studio until we get the release. St. Cyr can still out-shout me any time. But he's hooked. We —"

"Nick," Erika said, looking searchingly into his face. "What's happened?"

"Tell you tonight," Martin said hastily, hearing a distant bellow that might be the voice of St. Cyr approaching. "When I have time I'm going to sweep you off your feet. Did you know that I've worshipped you from afar all my life? But right now, get Watt out of the way. Hurry!"

Erika cast a glance of amazed bewilderment at him as he thrust her out of the door. Martin thought there was a certain element of pleasure in the surprise.

* * * * *

"Where is Tolliver?" The loud, annoyed roar of St. Cyr made Martin wince. The director was displeased, it appeared, because only in Costumes could a pair of trousers be found large enough to fit him. He took it as a personal affront. "What have you done with Tolliver?" he bellowed.

"Louder, please," Martin said insolently. "I can't hear you."

"DeeDee," St. Cyr shouted, whirling toward the lovely star, who hadn't stirred from her rapturous admiration of DeeDee in technicolor overhead. "Where is Tolliver?"

Martin started. He had quite forgotten DeeDee.

"You don't know, do you, DeeDee?" he prompted quickly.

"Shut up," St. Cyr snapped. "Answer me, you —" He added a brisk polysyllable in Mixo-Lydian, with the desired effect. DeeDee wrinkled her flawless brow.

"Tolliver went away, I think. I've got it mixed up with the picture. He went home to meet Nick Martin, didn't he?"

"See?" Martin interrupted, relieved. "No use expecting DeeDee to —"

"But Martin is *here*!" St. Cyr shouted. "Think, think!"

"Was the contract release in the rushes?" DeeDee asked vaguely.

"A contract release?" St. Cyr roared. "What is this? Never will I permit it, never, never, never! DeeDee, answer me-where has Watt gone?"

"He went somewhere with that agent," DeeDee said. "Or was that in the rushes too?"

"But where, where, where?"

"They went to Atlantis," DeeDee announced with an air of faint triumph.

"No!" shouted St. Cyr. "That was the *picture*! The mermaid came from Atlantis, not Watt!"

"Tolliver didn't say he was coming from Atlantis," DeeDee murmured, unruffled. "He said he was going to Atlantis. Then he was going to meet Nick Martin at his house tonight and give him his contract release."

"When?" St. Cyr demanded furiously. "Think, DeeDee? What time did —"

"DeeDee," Martin said, stepping forward with suave confidence, "you can't remember a thing, can you?" But DeeDee was too subnormal to react even to a Disraeli-matrix. She merely smiled placidly at him.

"Out of my way, you writer!" roared St. Cyr, advancing upon Martin. "You will get no contract release! You do not waste St. Cyr's time and get away with it! This I will not endure. I fix you as I fixed Ed Cassidy!"

Martin drew himself up and froze St. Cyr with an insolent smile. His hand toyed with an imaginary monocle. Golden periods were hanging at the end of his tongue. There only remained to hypnotize St. Cyr as he had hypnotized Watt. He drew a deep breath to unlease the floods of his eloquence —

And St. Cyr, also too subhuman to be impressed by urbanity, hit Martin a clout on the jaw. It could never have happened in the British Parliament.

CHAPTER III

When the robot walked into Martin's office that evening, he, or it, went directly to the desk, unscrewed the bulb from the lamp, pressed the switch, and stuck his finger into the socket. There was a crackling flash. Eniac withdrew his finger and shook his metallic head violently.

"I needed that," he sighed. "I've been on the go all day, by the Kaldekooz time-scale. Paleolithic, Neolithic, Technological—I don't even know what time it is. Well, how's your ecological adjustment getting on?"

Martin rubbed his chin thoughtfully.

"Badly," he said. "Tell me, did Disraeli, as Prime Minister, ever have any dealings with a country called Mixo-Lydia?"

"I have no idea," said the robot. "Why do you ask?"

"Because my environment hauled back and took a poke at my jaw," Martin said shortly.

"Then you provoked it," Eniac countered. "A crisis—a situation of stress-always brings a man's dominant trait to the fore, and Disraeli was dominantly courageous. Under stress, his courage became insolence. But he was intelligent enough to arrange his environment so insolence would be countered on the semantic level. Mixo-Lydia, eh? I place it vaguely, some billions of years ago, when it was inhabited by giant white apes. Or-oh, now I remember. It's an encysted medieval survival, isn't it?"

Martin nodded.

"So is this movie studio," the robot said. "Your trouble is that you've run up against somebody who's got a better optimum ecological adjustment than you have. That's it. This studio environment is just emerging from medievalism, so it can easily slip back into that plenum when an optimum medievalist exerts pressure. Such types caused the Dark Ages. Well, you'd better change your environment to a neo-technological one, where the Disraeli matrix can be successfully pro-survival. In your era, only a few archaic social-encystments like this studio are feudalistic, so go somewhere else. It takes a feudalist to match a feudalist."

"But I can't go somewhere else," Martin complained. "Not without my contract release. I was supposed to pick it up tonight, but St. Cyr found out what was happening, and he'll throw a monkey-wrench in the works if he has to knock me out again to do it. I'm due at Watt's place now, but St. Cyr's already there —"

"Spare me the trivia," the robot said, raising his hand. "As for this St. Cyr, if he's a medieval character-type, obviously he'll knuckle under only to a stronger man of his own kind."

"How would Disraeli have handled this?" Martin demanded.

"Disraeli would never have got into such a situation in the first place," the robot said unhelpfully. "The ecologizer can give you the ideal ecological differential, but only for your own type, because otherwise it wouldn't be your optimum. Disraeli would have been a failure in Russia in Ivan's time."

"Would you mind clarifying that?" Martin asked thoughtfully.

"Certainly," the robot said with great rapidity. "It all depends on the threshold-response-time of the memory-circuits in the brain, if you assume the identity of the basic chromosome-pattern. The strength of neuronic activation varies in inverse proportion to the quantative memory factor. Only actual experience could give you Disraeli's memories, but your re-activity-thresholds have been altered until perception and emotional-indices approximate the Disraeli ratio."

"Oh," Martin said. "But how would *you*, say, assert yourself against a medieval steam-shovel?"

"By plugging my demountable brain into a larger steam-shovel," Eniac told him.

* * * * *

Martin seemed pensive. His hand rose, adjusting an invisible monocle, while a look of perceptive imagination suddenly crossed his face.

"You mentioned Russia in Ivan's time," he said. "Which Ivan would that be? Not, by any chance —?"

"Ivan the Fourth. Very well adjusted to his environment he was, too. However, enough of this chit-chat. Obviously you'll be one of the failures in our experiment, but our aim is to strike an average, so if you'll put the ecologizer on your —"

"That was Ivan the Terrible, wasn't it?" Martin interrupted. "Look here, could you impress the character-matrix of Ivan the Terrible on my brain?"

"That wouldn't help you a bit," the robot said. "Besides, it's not the purpose of the experiment. Now —"

"One moment. Disraeli can't cope with a medievalist like St. Cyr on his own level, but if I had Ivan the Terrible's reactive thresholds, I'll bet I could throw a bluff that might do the trick. Even though St. Cyr's bigger than I am, he's got a veneer of civilization ... now wait. He trades on that. He's always dealt with people who are too civilized to use his own methods. The trick would be to call his bluff. And Ivan's the man who could do it."

"But you don't understand."

"Didn't everybody in Russia tremble with fear at Ivan's name?"

"Yes, in —"

"Very well, then," Martin said triumphantly. "You're going to impress the character-matrix, of Ivan the Terrible on my mind, and then I'm going to put the bite on St. Cyr, the way Ivan would have done it. Disraeli's simply too civilized. Size is a factor, but character's more important. I don't *look* like Disraeli, but people have been reacting to me as though I were George Arliss down to the spit-curl. A good big man can always lick a good little man. But St. Cyr's never been up against a really uncivilized little man-one who'd gladly rip out an enemy's heart with his bare hands." Martin nodded briskly. "St. Cyr will back down —I've found that out. But it would take somebody like Ivan to make him stay all the way down."

"If you think I'm going to impress Ivan's matrix on you, you're wrong," the robot said.

"You couldn't be talked into it?"

"I," said Eniac, "am a robot, semantically adjusted. Of course you couldn't talk me into it."

Perhaps not, Martin reflected, but Disraeli-hm-m. "Man is a machine." Why, Disraeli was the one person in the world ideally fitted for robot-coercion. To him, men *were* machines-and what was Eniac?

"Let's talk this over —" Martin began, absently pushing the desk-lamp toward the robot. And then the golden tongue that had swayed empires was loosed....

"You're not going to like this," the robot said dazedly, sometime later. "Ivan won't do at ... oh, you've got me all confused. You'll have to eyeprint a —" He began to pull out of his sack the helmet and the quarter-mile of red ribbon.

"To tie up my bonny grey brain," Martin said, drunk with his own rhetoric. "Put it on my head. That's right. Ivan the Terrible, remember. I'll fix St. Cyr's Mixo-Lydian wagon."

"Differential depends on environment as much as on heredity," the robot muttered, clapping the helmet on Martin's head. "Though naturally Ivan wouldn't have had the Tsardom environment without his particular heredity, involving Helena Glinska-there!" He removed the helmet.

"But nothing's happening," Martin said. "I don't feel any different."

"It'll take a few moments. This isn't your basic character-pattern, remember, as Disraeli's was. Enjoy yourself while you can. You'll get the Ivan-effect soon enough." He shouldered the sack and headed uncertainly for the door.

"Wait," Martin said uneasily. "Are you sure —"

"Be quiet. I forgot something-some formality-now I'm all confused. Well, I'll think of it later, or earlier, as the case may be. I'll see you in twelve hours —I hope."

The robot departed. Martin shook his head tentatively from side to side. Then he got up and followed Eniac to the door. But there was no sign of the robot, except for a diminishing whirlwind of dust in the middle of the corridor.

Something began to happen in Martin's brain....

Behind him, the telephone rang.

Martin heard himself gasp with pure terror. With a sudden, impossible, terrifying, absolute certainty he *knew* who was telephoning.

Assassins!

* * * * *

"Yes, Mr. Martin," said Tolliver Watt's butler to the telephone. "Miss Ashby is here. She is with Mr. Watt and Mr. St. Cyr at the moment, but I will give her your message. You are detained. And she is to call for you-where?"

"The broom-closet on the second floor of the Writers' Building," Martin said in a quavering voice. "It's the only one near a telephone with a long enough cord so I could take the phone in here with me. But I'm not at all certain that I'm safe. I don't like the looks of that broom on my left."

"Sir?"

"Are you *sure* you're Tolliver Watt's butler?" Martin demanded nervously.

"Quite sure, Mr. —eh-Mr. Martin."

"I *am* Mr. Martin," cried Martin with terrified defiance. "By all the laws of God and man, Mr. Martin I am and Mr. Martin I will remain, in spite of all attempts by rebellious dogs to depose me from my rightful place."

"Yes, sir. The broom-closet, you say, sir?"

"The broom-closet. Immediately. But swear not to tell another soul, no matter how much you're threatened. I'll protect you."

"Very well, sir. Is that all?"

"Yes. Tell Miss Ashby to hurry. Hang up now. The line may be tapped. I have enemies."

There was a click. Martin replaced his own receiver and furtively surveyed the broom-closet. He told himself that this was ridiculous. There was nothing to be afraid of, was there? True, the broom-closet's narrow walls were closing in upon him alarmingly, while the ceiling descended....

Panic-stricken, Martin emerged from the closet, took a long breath, and threw back his shoulders. "N-not a thing to be afraid of," he said. "Who's afraid?" Whistling, he began to stroll down the hall toward the staircase, but midway agoraphobia overcame him, and his nerve broke.

He ducked into his own office and sweated quietly in the dark until he had mustered up enough courage to turn on a lamp.

The Encyclopedia Britannica, in its glass-fronted cabinet, caught his eye. With noiseless haste, Martin secured *Italy* to *Lord* and opened the volume at his desk. Something, obviously, was very, very wrong. The robot had said that Martin wasn't going to like being Ivan the Terrible, come to think of it. But was Martin wearing Ivan's character-matrix? Perhaps he'd got somebody else's matrix by mistake-that of some arrant coward. Or maybe the Mad Tsar of Russia had really been called Ivan the Terrified. Martin flipped the rustling pages nervously. Ivan, Ivan-here it was.

Son of Helena Glinska ... married Anastasia Zakharina-Koshkina ... private life unspeakably abominable ... memory astonishing, energy indefatigable, ungovernable fury-great natural ability, political foresight, anticipated the ideals of Peter the Great-Martin shook his head.

Then he caught his breath at the next line.

Ivan had lived in an atmosphere of apprehension, imagining that every man's hand was against him.

"Just like me," Martin murmured. "But-but there was more to Ivan than just cowardice. I don't understand."

"Differential," the robot had said, "depends on environment as much as on heredity. Though naturally Ivan wouldn't have had the Tsardom environment without his particular heredity."

Martin sucked in his breath sharply. Environment does make a difference. No doubt Ivan IV had been a fearful coward, but heredity plus environment had given Ivan the one great weapon that had enabled him to keep his cowardice a recessive trait.

Ivan the Terrible had been Tsar of all the Russias.

Give a coward a gun, and, while he doesn't stop being a coward, it won't show in the same way. He may act like a violent, aggressive tyrant instead. That, of course, was why Ivan had been ecologically successful-in his specialized environment. He'd never run up against many stresses that brought his dominant trait to the fore. Like Disraeli, he had been able to control his environment so that such stresses were practically eliminated.

Martin turned green.

Then he remembered Erika. Could he get Erika to keep St. Cyr busy, somehow, while he got his contract release from Watt? As long as he could avoid crises, he could keep his nerve from crumbling, but —*there were assassins everywhere*!

Erika was on her way to the lot by now. Martin swallowed.

He would meet her outside the studio. The broom-closet wasn't safe. He could be trapped there like a rat —

"Nonsense," Martin told himself with shivering firmness. "This isn't me. All I have to do is get a g-grip on m-myself. Come, now. Buck up. *Toujours l'audace!*"

But he went out of his office and downstairs very softly and cautiously. After all, one never knew. And when every man's hand was against one....

Quaking, the character-matrix of Ivan the Terrible stole toward a studio gate.

* * * * *

The taxi drove rapidly toward Bel-Air.

"But what were you doing up that tree?" Erika demanded.

Martin shook violently.

"A werewolf," he chattered. "And a vampire and a ghoul and —I *saw* them, I tell you. There I was at the studio gate, and they all came at me in a mob."

"But they were just coming back from dinner," Erika said. "You know Summit's doing night shooting on *Abbott and Costello Meet Everybody*. Karloff wouldn't hurt a fly."

"I kept telling myself that," Martin said dully, "but I was out of my mind with guilt and fear. You see, I'm an abominable monster. But it's not my fault. It's environmental. I grew up in brutal and degrading conditions-oh, look!" He pointed toward a traffic cop ahead. "The police! Traitors even in the palace guards!"

"Lady, is that guy nuts?" the cabbie demanded.

"Mad or sane, I am Nicholas Martin," Martin announced, with an abrupt volte face. He tried to stand up commandingly, bumped his head, screamed "*Assassins!*" and burrowed into a corner of the seat, panting horribly.

Erika gave him a thoughtful, worried look.

"Nick," she said, "How much have you had to drink? What's wrong?"

Martin shut his eyes and lay back against the cushions.

"Let me have a few minutes, Erika," he pleaded. "I'll be all right as soon as I recover from stress. It's only when I'm under stress that Ivan —"

"You can accept your contract release from Watt, can't you? Surely you'll be able to manage that."

"Of course," Martin said with feeble bravery. He thought it over and reconsidered. "If I can hold your hand," he suggested, taking no chances.

This disgusted Erika so much that for two miles there was no more conversation within the cab.

Erika had been thinking her own thoughts.

"You've certainly changed since this morning," she observed. "Threatening to make love to me, of all things. As if I'd stand for it. I'd like to see you try." There was a pause. Erika slid her eyes sidewise toward Martin. "I said I'd like to see you try," she repeated.

"Oh, you would, would you?" Martin said with hollow valor. He paused. Oddly enough his tongue, hitherto frozen stiff on one particular subject in Erika's presence, was now thoroughly loosened. Martin wasted no time on theory. Seizing his chance before a new stress might unexpectedly arise, he instantly poured out his heart to Erika, who visibly softened.

"But why didn't you ever say so before?" she asked.

"I can't imagine," Martin said. "Then you'll marry me?"

"But why were you acting so —"

"Will you marry me?"

"Yes," Erika said, and there was a pause. Martin moistened his lips, discovering that somehow he and Erika had moved close together. He was about to seal the bargain in the customary manner when a sudden thought struck him and made him draw back with a little start.

Erika opened her eyes.

"Ah —" said Martin. "Um. I just happened to remember. There's a bad flu epidemic in Chicago. Epidemics spread like wildfire, you know. Why, it could be in Hollywood by now-especially with the prevailing westerly winds."

"I'm damned if I'm going to be proposed to and not kissed," Erika said in a somewhat irritated tone. "You kiss me!"

"But I might give you bubonic plague," Martin said nervously. "Kissing spreads germs. It's a well-known fact."

"Nick!"

"Well —I don't know-when did you last have a cold?"

Erika pulled away from him and went to sit in the other corner.

"Ah," Martin said, after a long silence. "Erika?"

"Don't talk to me, you miserable man," Erika said. "You monster, you."

"I can't help it," Martin cried wildly. "I'll be a coward for twelve hours. It's not my fault. After eight tomorrow morning I'll —I'll walk into a lion-cage if you want, but tonight I'm as yellow as Ivan the Terrible! At least let me tell you what's been happening."

Erika said nothing. Martin instantly plunged into his long and improbable tale.

"I don't believe a word of it," Erika said, when he had finished. She shook her head sharply. "Just the same, I'm still your agent, and your career's still my responsibility. The first and only thing we have to do is get your contract release from Tolliver Watt. And that's *all* we're going to consider right now, do you hear?"

"But St. Cyr —"

"I'll do all the talking. You won't have to say a word. If St. Cyr tries to bully you, I'll handle him. But you've got to be there with me, or St. Cyr will make that an excuse to postpone things again. I know him."

"Now I'm under stress again," Martin said wildly. "I can't stand it. *I'm* not the Tsar of Russia."

"Lady," said the cab-driver, looking back, "if I was you, I'd sure as hell break off that engagement."

"Heads will roll for this," Martin said ominously.

* * * * *

"By mutual consent, agree to terminate ...yes," Watt said, affixing his name to the legal paper that lay before him on the desk. "That does it. But where in the world is that fellow Martin? He came in with you, I'm certain."

"Did he?" Erika asked, rather wildly. She too, was wondering how Martin had managed to vanish so miraculously from her side. Perhaps he had crept with lightning rapidity under the carpet. She forced her mind from the thought and reached for the contract release Watt was folding.

"Wait," St. Cyr said, his lower lip jutting. "What about a clause giving us an option on Martin's next play?"

Watt paused, and the director instantly struck home.

"Whatever it may be, I can turn it into a vehicle for DeeDee, eh, DeeDee?" He lifted a sausage finger at the lovely star, who nodded obediently.

"It's going to have an all-male cast," Erika said hastily. "And we're discussing contract releases, not options."

"He would give me an option if I had him here," St. Cyr growled, torturing his cigar horribly. "Why does everything conspire against an artist?" He waved a vast, hairy fist in the air. "Now I must break in a new writer, which is a great waste. Within a fortnight Martin would have been a St. Cyr writer. In fact, it is still possible."

"I'm afraid not, Raoul," Watt said resignedly. "You really shouldn't have hit Martin at the studio today."

"But-but he would not dare charge me with assault. In Mixo-Lydia —"

"Why, hello, Nick," DeeDee said, with a bright smile. "What are you hiding behind those curtains for?"

Every eye was turned toward the window draperies, just in time to see the white, terrified face of Nicholas Martin flip out of sight like a scared chipmunk's. Erika, her heart dropping, said hastily, "Oh, that isn't Nick. It doesn't look a bit like him. You made a mistake, DeeDee."

"Did I?" DeeDee asked, perfectly willing to agree.

"Certainly," Erika said, reaching for the contract release in Watt's hand. "Now if you'll just let me have this, I'll —"

"Stop!" cried St. Cyr in a bull's bellow. Head sunk between his heavy shoulders, he lumbered to the window and jerked the curtains aside.

"Ha!" the director said in a sinister voice. "Martin."

"It's a lie," Martin said feebly, making a desperate attempt to conceal his stress-triggered panic. "I've abdicated."

St. Cyr, who had stepped back a pace, was studying Martin carefully. Slowly the cigar in his mouth began to tilt upwards. An unpleasant grin widened the director's mouth.

He shook a finger under Martin's quivering nostrils.

"You!" he said. "Tonight it is a different tune, eh? Today you were drunk. Now I see it all. Valorous with pots, like they say."

"Nonsense," Martin said, rallying his courage by a glance at Erika. "Who say? Nobody but you would say a thing like that. Now what's this all about?"

"What were you doing behind that curtain?" Watt asked.

"*I* wasn't behind the curtain," Martin said, with great bravado. "*You* were. All of you. I was in front of the curtain. Can I help it if the whole lot of you conceal yourselves behind curtains in a library, like-like conspirators?" The word was unfortunately chosen. A panicky light flashed into Martin's eyes. "Yes, conspirators," he went on nervously. "You think I don't know, eh? Well, I do. You're all assassins, plotting and planning. So this is your headquarters, is it? All night your hired dogs have been at my heels, driving me like a wounded caribou to —"

"We've got to be going," Erika said desperately. "There's just time to catch the next carib-the next plane east." She reached for the contract release, but Watt suddenly put it in his pocket. He turned his chair toward Martin.

"Will you give us an option on your next play?" he demanded.

"Of course he will give us an option!" St. Cyr said, studying Martin's air of bravado with an experienced eye. "Also, there is to be no question of a charge of assault, for, if there is I will beat you. So it is in Mixo-Lydia. In fact, you do not even want a release from your contract, Martin. It is all a mistake. I will turn you into a St. Cyr writer, and all will be well. So. Now you will ask Tolliver to tear up that release, will you not —*ha*?"

"Of course you won't, Nick," Erika cried. "Say so!"

* * * * *

There was a pregnant silence. Watt watched with sharp interest. So did the unhappy Erika, torn between her responsibility as Martin's agent and her disgust at the man's abject cowardice. DeeDee watched too, her eyes very wide and a cheerful smile upon her handsome face. But the battle was obviously between Martin and Raoul St. Cyr.

Martin drew himself up desperately. Now or never he must force himself to be truly Terrible. Already he had a troubled expression, just like Ivan. He strove to look sinister too. An enigmatic smile played around his lips. For an instant he resembled the Mad Tsar of Russia, except, of course, that he was clean-shaven. With contemptuous, regal power Martin stared down the Mixo-Lydian.

"You will tear up that release and sign an agreement giving us option on your next play too, ha?" St. Cyr said-but a trifle uncertainly.

"I'll do as I please," Martin told him. "How would you like to be eaten alive by dogs?"

"I don't know, Raoul," Watt said. "Let's try to get this settled even if—"

"Do you want me to go over to Metro and take DeeDee with me?" St. Cyr cried, turning toward Watt. "He *will* sign!" And, reaching into an inner pocket for a pen, the burly director swung back toward Martin.

"*Assassin!*" cried Martin, misinterpreting the gesture.

A gloating smile appeared on St. Cyr's revolting features.

"Now we have him, Tolliver," he said, with heavy triumph, and these ominous words added the final stress to Martin's overwhelming burden. With a mad cry he rushed past St. Cyr, wrenched open a door, and fled.

From behind him came Erika's Valkyrie voice.

"Leave him alone! Haven't you done enough already? Now I'm going to get that contract release from you before I leave this room, Tolliver Watt, and I warn you, St. Cyr, if you—"

But by then Martin was five rooms away, and the voice faded. He darted on, hopelessly trying to make himself slow down and return to the scene of battle. The pressure was too strong. Terror hurled him down a corridor, into another room, and against a metallic object from which he rebounded, to find himself sitting on the floor looking up at Eniac Gamma the Ninety-Third.

"Ah, there you are," the robot said. "I've been searching all over space-time for you. You forgot to give me a waiver of responsibility when you talked me into varying the experiment. The Authorities would be in my gears if I didn't bring back an eyeprinted waiver when a subject's scratched by variance."

With a frightened glance behind him, Martin rose to his feet.

"What?" he asked confusedly. "Listen, you've got to change me back to myself. Everyone's trying to kill me. You're just in time. I can't wait twelve hours. Change me back to myself, quick!"

"Oh, I'm through with you," the robot said callously. "You're no longer a suitably unconditioned subject, after that last treatment you insisted on. I should have got the waiver from you then, but you got me all confused with Disraeli's oratory. Now here. Just hold this up to your left eye for twenty seconds." He extended a flat, glittering little metal disk. "It's already sensitized and filled out. It only needs your eyeprint. Affix it, and you'll never see me again."

Martin shrank away.

"But what's going to happen to me?" he quavered, swallowing.

"How should I know? After twelve hours, the treatment will wear off, and you'll be yourself again. Hold this up to your eye, now."

"I will if you'll change me back to myself," Martin haggled.

"I can't. It's against the rules. One variance is bad enough, even with a filed waiver, but two? Oh, no. Hold this up to your left eye —"

"No," Martin said with feeble firmness. "I won't."

Eniac studied him.

"Yes, you will," the robot said finally, "or I'll go boo at you."

Martin paled slightly, but he shook his head in desperate determination.

"No," he said doggedly. "Unless I get rid of Ivan's matrix right now, Erika will never marry me and I'll never get my contract release from Watt. All you have to do is put that helmet on my head and change me back to myself. Is that too much to ask?"

"Certainly, of a robot," Eniac said stiffly. "No more shilly-shallying. It's lucky you are wearing the Ivan-matrix, so I can impose my will on you. Put your eyeprint on this. Instantly!"

Martin rushed behind the couch and hid. The robot advanced menacingly. And at that moment, pushed to the last ditch, Martin suddenly remembered something.

He faced the robot.

*　*　*　*　*

"Wait," he said. "You don't understand. I can't eyeprint that thing. It won't work on me. Don't you realize that? It's supposed to take the eyeprint —"

" —of the rod-and-cone pattern of the retina," the robot said. "So —"

"So how can it do that unless I can keep my eye open for twenty seconds? My perceptive reaction-thresholds are Ivan's aren't they? I can't control the reflex of blinking. I've got a coward's synapses. And they'd force me to shut my eyes tight the second that gimmick got too close to them."

"Hold them open," the robot suggested. "With your fingers."

"My fingers have reflexes too," Martin argued, moving toward a sideboard. "There's only one answer. I've got to get drunk. If I'm half stupefied with liquor, my reflexes will be so slow I won't be able to shut my eyes. And don't try to use force, either. If I dropped dead with fear, how could you get my eyeprint then?"

"Very easily," the robot said. "I'd pry open your lids —"

Martin hastily reached for a bottle on the sideboard, and a glass. But his hand swerved aside and gripped, instead, a siphon of soda water.

" —only," Eniac went on, "the forgery might be detected."

Martin fizzled the glass full of soda and took a long drink.

"I won't be long getting drunk," he said, his voice thickening. "In fact, it's beginning to work already. See? I'm coöperating."

The robot hesitated.

"Well, hurry up about it," he said, and sat down.

Martin, about to take another drink, suddenly paused, staring at Eniac. Then, with a sharply indrawn breath, he lowered the glass.

"What's the matter now?" the robot asked. "Drink your-what is it?"

"It's whiskey," Martin told the inexperienced automaton, "but now I see it all. You've put poison in it. So that's your plan, is it? Well, I won't touch another drop, and now you'll never get my eyeprint. I'm no fool."

"Cog Almighty," the robot said, rising. "You poured that drink yourself. How could I have poisoned it? Drink!"

"I won't," Martin said, with a coward's stubbornness, fighting back the growing suspicion that the drink might really be toxic.

"You swallow that drink," Eniac commanded, his voice beginning to quiver slightly. "It's perfectly harmless."

"Then prove it!" Martin said cunningly. "Would you be willing to switch glasses? Would you drink this poisoned brew yourself?"

"How do you expect me to drink?" the robot demanded. "I —" He paused. "All right, hand me the glass," he said. "I'll take a sip. Then you've got to drink the rest of it."

"Aha!" Martin said. "You betrayed yourself that time. You're a robot. You can't drink, remember? Not the same way that I can, anyhow. Now I've got you trapped, you assassin. *There's* your brew." He pointed to a floor-lamp. "Do you dare to drink with me now, in your electrical fashion, or do you admit you are trying to poison me? Wait a minute, what am I saying? That wouldn't prove a —"

"Of course it would," the robot said hastily. "You're perfectly right, and it's very cunning of you. We'll drink together, and that will prove your whiskey's harmless-so you'll keep on drinking till your reflexes slow down, see?"

"Well," Martin began uncertainly, but the unscrupulous robot unscrewed a bulb from the floor lamp, pulled the switch, and inserted his finger into the empty socket, which caused a crackling flash. "There," the robot said. "It isn't poisoned, see?"

"You're not swallowing it," Martin said suspiciously. "You're holding it in your mouth —I mean your finger."

Eniac again probed the socket.

"Well, all right, perhaps," Martin said, in a doubtful fashion. "But I'm not going to risk your slipping a powder in my liquor, you traitor. You're going to keep up with me, drink for drink, until I can eyeprint that gimmick of yours-or else I stop drinking. But does sticking your finger in that lamp really prove my liquor isn't poisoned? I can't quite —"

"Of course it does," the robot said quickly. "I'll prove it. I'll do it again ...*f(t)*. Powerful DC, isn't it? Certainly it proves it. Keep drinking, now."

* * * * *

His gaze watchfully on the robot, Martin lifted his glass of club soda.

"*Fffff(t)!*" cried the robot, some time later, sketching a singularly loose smile on its metallic face.

"Best fermented mammoth's milk I ever tasted," Martin agreed, lifting his tenth glass of soda-water. He felt slightly queasy and wondered if he might be drowning.

"Mammoth's milk?" asked Eniac thickly. "What year is this?"

Martin drew a long breath. Ivan's capacious memory had served him very well so far. Voltage, he recalled, increased the frequency of the robot's thought-patterns and disorganized Eniac's memory-which was being proved before his eyes. But the crux of his plan was yet to come....

"The year of the great Hairy One, of course," Martin said briskly. "Don't you remember?"

"Then you —" Eniac strove to focus upon his drinking-companion. "You must be Mammoth-Slayer."

"That's it!" Martin cried. "Have another jolt. What about giving me the treatment now?"

"What treatment?"

Martin looked impatient. "You said you were going to impose the character-matrix of Mammoth-Slayer on my mind. You said *that* would insure my optimum ecological adjustment in this temporal phase, and nothing else would."

"Did I? But you're not Mammoth-Slayer," Eniac said confusedly. "Mammoth-Slayer was the son of the Great Hairy One. What's your mother's name?"

"The Great Hairy One," Martin replied, at which the robot grated its hand across its gleaming forehead.

"Have one more jolt," Martin suggested. "Now take out the ecologizer and put it on my head."

"Like this?" Eniac asked, obeying. "I keep feeling I've forgotten something important. *F (t).*"

Martin adjusted the crystal helmet on his skull. "Now," he commanded. "Give me the char-acter-matrix of Mammoth-Slayer, son of the Great Hairy One."

"Well-all right," Eniac said dizzily. The red ribbons swirled. There was a flash from the helmet. "There," the robot said. "It's done. It may take a few minutes to begin functioning, but then for twelve hours you'll-wait! Where are you going?"

But Martin had already departed.

The robot stuffed the helmet and the quarter-mile of red ribbon back for the last time. He lurched to the floor-lamp, muttering something about one for the road. Afterward, the room lay empty. A fading murmur said, "$F(t)$."

* * * * *

"Nick!" Erika gasped, staring at the figure in the doorway. "Don't stand like that! You frighten me!"

Everyone in the room looked up abruptly at her cry, and so were just in time to see a horrifying change take place in Martin's shape. It was an illusion, of course, but an alarming one. His knees slowly bent until he was half-crouching, his shoulders slumped as though bowed by the weight of enormous back and shoulder muscles, and his arms swung forward until their knuckles hung perilously near the floor.

Nicholas Martin had at last achieved a personality whose ecological norm would put him on a level with Raoul St. Cyr.

"Nick!" Erika quavered.

Slowly Martin's jaw protruded till his lower teeth were hideously visible. Gradually his eyelids dropped until he was peering up out of tiny, wicked sockets. Then, slowly, a perfectly shocking grin broadened Mr. Martin's mouth.

"Erika," he said throatily. "Mine!"

And with that, he shambled forward, seized the horrified girl in his arms, and bit her on the ear.

"Oh, Nick," Erika murmured, closing her eyes. "Why didn't you ever-no, no, *no*! Nick! Stop it! The contract release. We've got to-Nick, what are you doing?" She snatched at Martin's departing form, but too late.

For all his ungainly and unpleasant gait, Martin covered ground fast. Almost instantly he was clambering over Watt's desk as the most direct route to that startled tycoon. DeeDee looked on, a little surprised. St. Cyr lunged forward.

"In Mixo-Lydia —" he began. "Ha! So!" He picked up Martin and threw him across the room.

"Oh, you beast," Erika cried, and flung herself upon the director, beating at his brawny chest. On second thought, she used her shoes on his shins with more effect. St. Cyr, no gentleman, turned her around, pinioned her arms behind her, and glanced up at Watt's alarmed cry.

"Martin! What are you doing?"

There was reason for his inquiry. Apparently unhurt by St. Cyr's toss, Martin had hit the floor, rolled over and over like a ball, knocked down a floor-lamp with a crash, and uncurled, with an unpleasant expression on his face. He rose crouching, bandy-legged, his arms swinging low, a snarl curling his lips.

"You take my mate?" the pithecanthropic Mr. Martin inquired throatily, rapidly losing all touch with the twentieth century. It was a rhetorical question. He picked up the lamp-standard —he did not have to bend to do it-tore off the silk shade as he would have peeled foliage from a tree-limb, and balanced the weapon in his hand. Then he moved forward, carrying the lamp-standard like a spear.

"I," said Martin, "kill."

He then endeavored, with the most admirable single-heartedness, to carry out his expressed intention. The first thrust of the blunt, improvised spear rammed into St. Cyr's solar plexus and drove him back against the wall with a booming thud. This seemed to be what Martin wanted. Keeping one end of his spear pressed into the director's belly, he crouched lower, dug his toes into the rug, and did his very best to drill a hole in St. Cyr.

"Stop it!" cried Watt, flinging himself into the conflict. Ancient reflexes took over. Martin's arm shot out. Watt shot off in the opposite direction.

The lamp broke.

Martin looked pensively at the pieces, tentatively began to bite one, changed his mind, and looked at St. Cyr instead. The gasping director, mouthing threats, curses and objections, drew himself up, and shook a huge fist at Martin.

"I," he announced, "shall kill you with my bare hands. Then I go over to MGM with DeeDee. In Mixo-Lydia —"

Martin lifted his own fists toward his face. He regarded them. He unclenched them slowly, while a terrible grin spread across his face. And then, with every tooth showing, and with the hungry gleam of a mad tiger in his tiny little eyes, he lifted his gaze to St. Cyr's throat.

Mammoth-Slayer was not the son of the Great Hairy One for nothing.

*　*　*　*　*

Martin sprang.

So did St. Cyr-in another direction, screaming with sudden terror. For, after all, he was only a medievalist. The feudal man is far more civilized than the so-called man of Mammoth-Slayer's primordially direct era, and as a man recoils from a small but murderous wildcat, so St. Cyr fled in sudden civilized horror from an attacker who was, literally, afraid of nothing.

He sprang through the window and, shrieking, vanished into the night.

Martin was taken by surprise. When Mammoth-Slayer leaped at an enemy, the enemy leaped at him too, and so Martin's head slammed against the wall with disconcerting force. Dimly he heard diminishing, terrified cries. Laboriously he crawled to his feet and set back against the wall, snarling, quite ready....

"Nick!" Erika's voice called. "Nick, it's me! Stop it! *Stop it!* DeeDee —"

"Ugh?" Martin said thickly, shaking his head. "Kill." He growled softly, blinking through red-rimmed little eyes at the scene around him. It swam back slowly into focus. Erika was struggling with DeeDee near the window.

"You let me go," DeeDee cried. "Where Raoul goes, I go."

"DeeDee!" pleaded a new voice. Martin glanced aside to see Tolliver Watt crumpled in a corner, a crushed lamp-shade half obscuring his face.

With a violent effort Martin straightened up. Walking upright seemed unnatural, somehow, but it helped submerge Mammoth-Slayer's worst instincts. Besides, with St. Cyr gone, stresses were slowly subsiding, so that Mammoth-Slayer's dominant trait was receding from the active foreground.

Martin tested his tongue cautiously, relieved to find he was still capable of human speech.

"Uh," he said. "Arrgh ... ah. Watt."

Watt blinked at him anxiously through the lamp-shade.

"Urgh ... Ur-release," Martin said, with a violent effort. "Contract release. Gimme."

Watt had courage. He crawled to his feet, removing the lamp-shade.

"Contract release!" he snapped. "You madman! Don't you realize what you've done? DeeDee's walking out on me. DeeDee, don't go. We will bring Raoul back —"

"Raoul told me to quit if he quit," DeeDee said stubbornly.

"You don't have to do what St. Cyr tells you," Erika said, hanging onto the struggling star.

"Don't I?" DeeDee asked, astonished. "Yes, I do. I always have."

"DeeDee," Watt said frantically, "I'll give you the finest contract on earth — a ten-year con-tract-look, here it is." He tore out a well-creased document. "All you have to do is sign, and you can have anything you want. Wouldn't you like that?"

"Oh, yes," DeeDee said. "But Raoul wouldn't like it." She broke free from Erika.

"Martin!" Watt told the playwright frantically, "Get St. Cyr back. Apologize to him. I don't care how, but get him back! If you don't, I —I'll never give you your release."

Martin was observed to slump slightly-perhaps with hopelessness. Then, again, perhaps not.

"I'm sorry," DeeDee said. "I liked working for you, Tolliver. But I have to do what Raoul says, of course." And she moved toward the window.

Martin had slumped further down, till his knuckles quite brushed the rug. His angry little eyes, glowing with baffled rage, were fixed on DeeDee. Slowly his lips peeled back, exposing every tooth in his head.

"You," he said, in an ominous growl.

DeeDee paused, but only briefly.

* * * * *

Then the enraged roar of a wild beast reverberated through the room. *"You come back!"* bellowed the infuriated Mammoth-Slayer, and with one agile bound sprang to the window, seized DeeDee and slung her under one arm. Wheeling, he glared jealously at the shrinking Watt and reached for Erika. In a trice he had the struggling forms of both girls captive, one under each arm. His wicked little eyes glanced from one to another. Then, playing no favorites, he bit each quickly on the ear.

"Nick!" Erika cried. "How dare you!"

"Mine," Mammoth-Slayer informed her hoarsely.

"You bet I am," Erika said, "but that works both ways. Put down that hussy you've got under your other arm."

Mammoth-Slayer was observed to eye DeeDee doubtfully.

"Well," Erika said tartly, "make up your mind."

"Both," said the uncivilized playwright. "Yes."

"No!" Erika said.

"Yes," DeeDee breathed in an entirely new tone. Limp as a dishrag, the lovely creature hung from Martin's arm and gazed up at her captor with idolatrous admiration.

"Oh, you hussy," Erika said. "What about St. Cyr?"

"Him," DeeDee said scornfully. "He hasn't got a thing, the sissy. I'll never look at him again." She turned her adoring gaze back to Martin.

"Pah," the latter grunted, tossing DeeDee into Watt's lap. "Yours. Keep her." He grinned approvingly at Erika. "Strong she. Better."

Both Watt and DeeDee remained motionless, staring at Martin.

"You," he said, thrusting a finger at DeeDee. "You stay with him. Ha?" He indicated Watt.

DeeDee nodded in slavish adoration.

"You sign contract?"

Nod.

Martin looked significantly into Watt's eyes. He extended his hand.

"The contract release," Erika explained, upside-down. "Give it to him before he pulls your head off."

Slowly Watt pulled the contract release from his pocket and held it out. But Martin was already shambling toward the window. Erika reached back hastily and snatched the document.

"That was a wonderful act," she told Nick, as they reached the street. "Put me down now. We can find a cab some —"

"No act," Martin growled. "Real. Till tomorrow. After that —" He shrugged. "But tonight, Mammoth-Slayer." He attempted to climb a palm tree, changed his mind, and shambled on, carrying the now pensive Erika. But it was not until a police car drove past that Erika screamed....

* * * * *

"I'll bail you out tomorrow," Erika told Mammoth-Slayer, struggling between two large patrolmen.

Her words were drowned in an infuriated bellow.

Thereafter events blurred, to solidify again for the irate Mammoth-Slayer only when he was thrown in a cell, where he picked himself up with a threatening roar. "I kill!" he announced, seizing the bars.

"Arrrgh!"

"Two in one night," said a bored voice, moving away outside. "Both in Bel-Air, too. Think they're hopped up? We couldn't get a coherent story out of either one."

The bars shook. An annoyed voice from one of the bunks said to shut up, and added that there had been already enough trouble from nincompoops without-here it paused, hesitated, and uttered a shrill, sharp, piercing cry.

Silence prevailed, momentarily, in the cell-block as Mammoth-Slayer, son of the Great Hairy One, turned slowly to face Raoul St. Cyr.

Where the World is Quiet

The life of an anthropologist is no doubt filled much of the time with the monotonous routine of carefully assembling powdery relics of ancient races and civilizations. But White's lone Peruvian odyssey was most unusual. A story pseudonymously penned by one of the greats in the genre.

Fra Rafael saw strange things, impossible things. Then there was the mystery of the seven young virginal girls of Huascan.

Fra Rafael drew the llama-wool blanket closer about his narrow shoulders, shivering in the cold wind that screamed down from Huascan. His face held great pain. I rose, walked to the door of the hut and peered through fog at the shadowy haunted lands that lifted toward the sky-the Cordilleras that make a rampart along Peru's eastern border.

"There's nothing," I said. "Only the fog, Fra Rafael."

He made the sign of the cross on his breast. "It is the fog that brings the-the terror," he said. "I tell you, *Señor* White, I have seen strange things these last few months-impossible things. You are a scientist. Though we are not of the same religion, you also know that there are powers not of this earth."

I didn't answer, so he went on: "Three months ago it began, after the earthquake. A native girl disappeared. She was seen going into the mountains, toward Huascan along the Pass, and she did not come back. I sent men out to find her. They went up the Pass, found the fog grew thicker and thicker until they were blind and could see nothing. Fear came to them and they fled back down the mountain. A week later another girl vanished. We found her footprints."

"The same canyon?"

"*Si*, and the same result. Now seven girls have gone, one after the other, all in the same way. And I, *Señor* White —" Fra Rafael's pale, tired face was sad as he glanced down at the stumps of his legs —"I could not follow, as you see. Four years ago an avalanche crippled me. My bishop told me to return to Lima, but I prevailed on him to let me remain here for these natives are my people, *Señor*. They know and trust me. The loss of my legs has not altered that."

I nodded. "I can see the difficulty now, though."

"Exactly. I cannot go to Huascan and find out what has happened to the girls. The natives-well, I chose four of the strongest and bravest and asked them to take me up the Pass. I thought that I could overcome their superstitions. But I was not successful."

"How far did you go?" I asked.

"A few miles, not more than that. The fog grew thicker, until we were blinded by it, and the way was dangerous. I could not make the men go on." Fra Rafael closed his eyes wearily. "They talked of old Inca gods and devils-Manco Capac and Oello Huaco, the Children of the Sun. They are very much afraid, *Señor* White. They huddle together like sheep and believe that an ancient god has returned and is taking them away one by one. And-one by one they *are* taken."

"Only young girls," I mused. "And no coercion is used, apparently. What's up toward Huascan?"

"Nothing but wild llamas and the condors. And snow, cold, desolation. These are the Andes, my friend."

"Okay," I said. "It sounds interesting. As an anthropologist I owe it to the Foundation to investigate. Besides, I'm curious. Superficially, there is nothing very strange about the affair. Seven girls have disappeared in the unusually heavy fogs we've had ever since the earthquake. Nothing more."

I smiled at him. "However, I think I'll take a look around and see what's so attractive about Huascan."

"I shall pray for you," he said. "Perhaps-well, *Señor,* for all the loss of my legs, I am not a weak man. I can stand much hardship. I can ride a burro."

"I don't doubt your willingness, Fra Rafael," I said. "But it's necessary to be practical. It's dangerous and it's cold up there. Your presence would only handicap me. Alone, I can go faster-remember, I don't know how far I'll have to travel."

The priest sighed. "I suppose you are right. When —"

"Now. My burro's packed."

"Your porters?"

"They won't go," I said wryly. "They've been talking to your villagers. It doesn't matter. I'll go it alone." I put out my hand, and Fra Rafael gripped it strongly.

"*Vaya con Dios,*" he said.

I went out into the bright Peruvian sunlight. The Indios were standing in straggling knots, pretending not to watch me. My porters were nowhere in evidence. I grinned, yelled a sardonic goodbye, and started to lead the burro toward the Pass.

The fog vanished as the sun rose, but it still lay in the mountain canyons toward the west. A condor circled against the sky. In the thin, sharp air the sound of a distant rock-fall was distinctly audible.

White Huascan towered far away. A shadow fell on me as I entered the Pass. The burro plodded on, patient and obedient. I felt a little chill; the fog began to thicken.

Yes, the Indios had talked to me. I knew their language, their old religion. Bastard descendants of the Incas, they still preserved a deep-rooted belief in the ancient gods of their ancient race, who had fallen with Huayna Capac, the Great Inca, a year before Pizarro came raging into Peru. I knew the Quichua-the old tongue of the mother race-and so I learned more than I might have otherwise.

Yet I had not learned much. The Indios said that *something* had come into the mountains near Huascan. They were willing to talk about it, but they knew little. They shrugged with apathetic fatalism. *It* called the young virgins, no doubt for a sacrifice. *Quien sabe?* Certainly the strange, thickening fog was not of this earth. Never before in the history of mankind had there been such a fog. It was, of course, the earthquake that had brought the-the Visitant. And it was folly to seek it out.

Well, I was an anthropologist and knew the value of even such slight clues as this. Moreover, my job for the Foundation was done. My specimens had been sent through to Callao by pack-train, and my notes were safe with Fra Rafael. Also, I was young and the lure of far places and their mysteries was hot in my blood. I hoped I'd find something odd-even dangerous-at Huascan.

I was young. Therefore, somewhat of a fool....

The first night I camped in a little cave, sheltered from the wind and snug enough in my fleece-lined sleeping-bag. There were no insects at this height. It was impossible to make a fire for there was no wood. I worried a bit about the burro freezing in the night.

But he survived, and I repacked him the next morning with rather absurd cheerfulness. The fog was thick, yes, but not impenetrable.

There were tracks in the snow where the wind had not covered them. A girl had left the village the day before my arrival, which made my task all the easier. So I went up into that vast, desolate silence, the fog closing in steadily, getting thicker and thicker, the trail getting narrower until at last it was a mere track.

And then I was moving blind. I had to feel my way, step by step, leading the burro. Occasional tracks showed through the mist, showed that the native girl had walked swiftly-had run in places-so I assumed that the fog was less dense when she had come by this way. As it happened, I was quite wrong about that....

We were on a narrow path above a gorge when I lost the burro. I heard a scrambling and clashing of hoofs on rock behind me. The rope jerked out of my hand and the animal cried out almost articulately as it went over. I stood frozen, pressing against the stone, listening to the sound of the burro's fall. Finally the distant noise died in a faint trickling of snow and gravel that faded into utter silence. So thick was the fog that I had seen nothing.

I felt my way back to where the path had crumbled and rotten rock had given way under the burro's weight. It was possible for me to retrace my steps, but I did not. I was sure that my destination could not be much further. A lightly clad native girl could not have gone so far as Huascan itself. No, probably that day I would reach my goal.

So I went on, feeling my way through the thick silent fog. I was able to see only a few inches ahead of me for hours. Then, abruptly the trail grew clearer. Until, at last I was moving in the shadowless, unearthly mist over hard-packed snow, following the clearly marked footprints of a girl's sandals.

Then they vanished without warning, those prints, and I stood hesitant, staring around. I could see nothing, but a brighter glow in the misty canopy overhead marked the sun's position.

I knelt and brushed away the snow with my hands, hoping to undo the wind's concealing work. But I found no more footprints. Finally I took my bearings as well as I could and ploughed ahead in the general direction the girl had been traveling.

My compass told me I was heading due north.

The fog was a living, sentient thing now, secretive, shrouding the secret that lay beyond its gray wall.

Suddenly I was conscious of a change. An electric tingle coursed through my body. Abruptly the fog-wall brightened. Dimly, as through a translucent pane, I could make out vague images ahead of me.

I began to move toward the images-and suddenly the fog was gone!

Before me lay a valley. Blue-white moss carpeted it except where reddish boulders broke the blueness. Here and there were trees-at least I assumed they were trees, despite their unfamiliar outline. They were like banyans, having dozens of trunks narrow as bamboo. Blue-leafed, they stood like immense bird-cages on the pallid moss. The fog closed in behind the valley and above it. It was like being in a huge sun-lit cavern.

I turned my head, saw a gray wall behind me. Beneath my feet the snow was melting and running in tiny, trickling rivulets among the moss. The air was warm and stimulating as wine.

A strange and abrupt change. Impossibly strange! I walked toward one of the trees, stopped at a reddish boulder to examine it. And surprise caught at my throat. It was an artifact —a crumbling ruin, the remnant of an ancient structure whose original appearance I could not fathom. The stone seemed iron-hard. There were traces of inscription on it, but eroded to illegibility. And I never did learn the history of those enigmatic ruins.... They did not originate on Earth.

There was no sign of the native girl, and the resilient moss retained no tracks. I stood there, staring around, wondering what to do now. I was tense with excitement. But there was little to see. Just that valley covering perhaps a half-mile before the fog closed in around it.

Beyond that —I did not know what lay beyond that.

I went on, into the valley, eyeing my surroundings curiously in the shadowless light that filtered through the shifting roof of fog. Foolishly, I expected to discover Incan artifacts. The crumbled red stones should have warned me. They were, I think, harder than metal, yet they had been here long enough for the elements to erode them into featureless shards. Had they been of earthly origin they would have antedated Mankind-antedated even the Neanderthaler man.

Curious how our minds are conditioned to run in anthropomorphic lines. I was, though I did not know it, walking through a land that had its beginnings outside the known universe. The blue trees hinted at that. The crimson ruins told me that clearly. The atmospheric conditions-the fog, the warmth high up in the Cordilleras-were certainly not natural. Yet I thought the explanation lay in some geological warp, volcanic activity, subterranean gas-vents....

My vision reached a half-mile, no farther. As I went on, the misty horizon receded. The valley was larger than I had imagined. It was like Elysium, where the shades of dead men stroll in the Garden of Proserpine. Streamlets ran through the blue moss at intervals, chill as death from the snowy plains hidden in the fog. "A sleepy world of streams...."

The ruins altered in appearance as I went on. The red blocks were still present, but there were now also remnants of other structures, made by a different culture, I thought.

The blue trees grew more numerous. Leafy vines covered most of them now, saffron-tinted, making each strange tree a little room, screened by the lattice of the vines. As I passed close to one a faint clicking sounded, incongruously like the tapping of typewriter keys, but muffled. I saw movement and turned, my hand going to the pistol in my belt.

The Thing came out of a tree-hut and halted, watching me. I *felt* it watching me-though *it had no eyes!*

It was a sphere of what seemed to be translucent plastic, glowing with shifting rainbow colors. And I sensed sentience-intelligence-in its horribly human attitude of watchful hesitation. Four feet in diameter it was, and featureless save for three ivory elastic tentacles that supported it and a fringe of long, whip-like cilia about its diameter-its waist, I thought.

It looked at me, eyeless and cryptic. The shifting colors crawled over the plastic globe. Then it began to roll forward on the three supporting tentacles with a queer, swift gliding motion. I stepped back, jerking out my gun and leveling it.

"Stop," I said, my voice shrill. "Stop!"

It stopped, quite as though it understood my words or the gesture of menace. The cilia fluttered about its spherical body. Bands of lambent color flashed. I could not rid myself of the curious certainty, that it was trying to communicate with me.

Abruptly it came forward again purposefully. I tensed and stepped back, holding the gun aimed. My finger was tightening on the trigger when the Thing stopped.

I backed off, nervously tense, but the creature did not follow. After I had got about fifty yards away it turned back and retreated into the hut-like structure in the banyan tree. After that I watched the trees warily as I passed them, but there were no other visitations of that nature.

Scientists are reluctant to relinquish their so-called logic. As I walked I tried to rationalize the creature, to explain it in the light of current knowledge. That it had been alive was certain. Yet it was not protoplasmic in nature. A plant, developed by mutation? Perhaps. But that theory did not satisfy me for the Thing had possessed intelligence, though of what order I did not know.

But there were the seven native girls, I reminded myself. My job was to find them, and quickly, too.

I did, at last, find them. Six of them, anyway. They were sitting in a row on the blue moss, facing one of the red blocks of stone, their backs toward me. As I mounted a little rise I saw them, motionless as bronze statues, and as rigid.

I went down toward them, tense with excitement, expectancy. Odd that six native girls, sitting in a row, should fill me with such feeling. They were so motionless that I wondered as I approached them, if they were dead....

But they were not. Nor were they-in the true sense of the word-alive.

I gripped one by the bare shoulder, found the flesh surprisingly cold and the girl seemed not to feel my touch. I swung her around to face me, and her black, empty eyes looked off into the far distance. Her lips were tightly compressed, slightly cyanosed. The pupils of her eyes were inordinately dilated, as if she was drugged.

Indian style, she squatted cross-legged, like the others. As I pulled her around, she toppled down on the moss, making no effort to stop herself. For a moment she lay there. Then with slow, puppet-like motions, she returned to her former position and resumed that blank staring into space.

I looked at the others. They were alike in their sleep-like withdrawal. It seemed as if their minds had been sucked out of them, that their very selves were elsewhere. It was a fantastic diagnosis, of course. But the trouble with those girls was nothing a physician could understand. It was psychic in nature, obviously.

I turned to the first one and slapped her cheeks. "Wake up!" I commanded. "You must obey me! Waken—"

But she gave no sign of feeling, of seeing. I lit a match, and her eyes focused on the flame. But the size of her pupils did not alter....

A shudder racked me. Then, abruptly I sensed movement behind me. I turned....

Over the blue moss the seventh Indio girl was coming toward us. "Miranda!" I said. "Can you hear me?" Fra Rafael had told me her name. Her feet, I saw, were bare and white frost-bite blotches marked them. But she did not seem to feel any pain as she walked.

Then I became aware that this was not a simple Indio girl. Something deep within my soul suddenly shrank back with instinctive revulsion. My skin seemed to crawl with a sort of terror. I began to shake so that it was difficult to draw my gun from its holster.

There was just this young native girl walking slowly toward me, her face quite expressionless, her black eyes fixed on emptiness. Yet she was not like other Indios, not like the six other girls sitting behind me. I can only liken her to a lamp in which a hot flame burned. The others were lamps that were dead, unlit.

The flame in her was not one that had been kindled on this earth, or in this universe, or in this space-time continuum, either. There was life in the girl who had been Miranda Valle-but it was not *human* life!

Some distant, skeptical corner of my brain told me that this was pure insanity, that I was deluded, hallucinated. Yes, I knew that. But it did not seem to matter. The girl who was walking so quietly across the blue yielding moss had wrapped about her, like an invisible, intangible veil, something of the alienage that men, through the eons, have called divinity. No mere human, I thought, could touch her.

* * * * *

But I felt fear, loathing-emotions not associated with divinity. I watched, knowing that presently she would look at me, would realize my presence. Then-well, my mind would not go beyond that point....

She came forward and quietly seated herself with the others, at the end of the line. Her body stiffened rigidly. Then, the veil of terror seemed to leave her, like a cloak falling away. Abruptly she was just an Indio girl, empty and drained as the others, mindless and motionless.

The girl beside her rose suddenly with a slow, fluid motion. And the crawling horror hit me again....The Alien Power had not left! It had merely transferred itself to another body!

And this second body was as dreadful to my senses as the first had been. In some subtly monstrous way its terror impressed itself on my brain, though all the while there was nothing overt, nothing *visibly* wrong. The strange landscape, bounded by fog, was not actually abnormal, considering its location, high in the Andes. The blue moss, the weird trees; they were strange, but possible. Even the seven native girls were a normal part of the scene. It was the sense of an alien presence that caused my terror—a fear of the unknown....

As the newly "possessed" girl rose, I turned and fled, deathly sick, feeling caught in the grip of nightmare. Once I stumbled and fell. As I scrambled wildly to my feet I looked back.

The girl was watching me, her face tiny and far away. Then, suddenly, abruptly it was close. She stood within a few feet of me! I had not moved nor seen her move, but we were all close together again-the seven girls and I....

Hypnosis? Something of that sort. She had drawn me back to her, my mind blacked out and unresisting. I could not move. I could only stand motionless while that Alien being dwelling within human flesh reached out and thrust frigid fingers into my soul. I could feel my mind laid open, spread out like a map before the inhuman gaze that scanned it. It was blasphemous and shameful, and I could not move or resist!

I was flung aside as the psychic grip that held me relaxed. I could not think clearly. That remote delving into my brain had made me blind, sick, frantic. I remember running....

But I remember very little of what followed. There are vague pictures of blue moss and twisted trees, of coiling fog that wrapped itself about me, trying futilely to hold me back. And always there was the sense of a dark and nameless horror just beyond vision, hidden from me-though I was not hidden from its eyeless gaze!

I remember reaching the wall of fog, saw it loomed before me, plunged into it, raced through cold grayness, snow crunching beneath my boots. I recall emerging again into that misty valley of Abaddon....

When I regained complete consciousness I was with Lhar.

A coolness as of limpid water moved through my mind, cleansing it, washing away the horror, soothing and comforting me. I was lying on my back looking up at an arabesque pattern of blue and saffron; gray-silver light filtered through a lacy, filigree. I was still weak but the blind terror no longer gripped me.

I was inside a hut formed by the trunks of one of the banyan-like trees. Slowly, weakly I rose on one elbow. The room was empty except for a curious flower that grew from the dirt floor beside me. I looked at it dazedly.

And so I met Lhar.... She was of purest white, the white of alabaster, but with a texture and warmth that stone does not have. In shape-well, she seemed to be a great flower, an unopened tulip-like blossom five feet or so tall. The petals were closely enfolded, concealing whatever sort of body lay hidden beneath, and at the base was a convoluted pedestal that gave the odd impression of a ruffled, tiny skirt. Even now I cannot describe Lhar coherently. A flower, yes-but very much more than that. Even in that first glimpse I knew that Lhar was more than just a flower....

I was not afraid of her. She had saved me, I knew, and I felt complete trust in her. I lay back as she spoke to me telepathically, her words and thoughts forming within my brain....

"You are well now, though still weak. But it is useless for you to try to escape from this valley. No one can escape. The Other has powers I do not know, and those powers will keep you here."

I said, "You are —?"

A name formed within my mind. "Lhar. I am not of your world."

A shudder shook her. And her distress forced itself on me. I stood up, swaying with weakness. Lhar drew back, moving with a swaying, bobbing gait oddly like a curtsey.

Behind me a clicking sounded. I turned, saw the many-colored sphere force itself through the banyan-trunks. Instinctively my hand went to my gun. But a thought from Lhar halted me.

"It will not harm you. It is my servant." She hesitated, groping for a word. "A machine. A robot. It will not harm you."

I said, "Is it intelligent?"

"Yes. But it is not alive. Our people made it. We have many such machines."

The robot swayed toward me, the rim of cilia flashing and twisting. Lhar said, "It speaks thus, without words or thought...." She paused, watching the sphere, and I sensed dejection in her manner.

The robot turned to me. The cilia twisted lightly about my arm, tugging me toward Lhar. I said, "What does it want?"

"It knows that I am dying," Lhar said.

That shocked me. "Dying? No!"

"It is true. Here in this alien world I do not have my usual food. So I will die. To survive I need the blood of mammals. But there are none here save those seven the Other has taken. And I cannot use them for they are now spoiled."

I didn't ask Lhar what sort of mammals she had in her own world. "That's what the robot wanted when it tried to stop me before, isn't it?"

"He wanted you to help me, yes. But you are weak from the shock you have had. I cannot ask you —"

I said, "How much blood do you need?"

At her answer, I said, "All right. You saved my life; I must do the same for you. I can spare that much blood easily. Go ahead."

She bowed toward me, a fluttering white flame in the dimness of the tree-room. A tendril flicked out from among her petals, wrapped itself about my arm. It felt cool, gentle as a woman's hand. I felt no pain.

"You must rest now," Lhar said. "I will go away but I shall not be long."

The robot clicked and chattered, shifting on its tentacle legs. I watched it, saying, "Lhar, this can't be true. Why am I —believing impossible things?"

"I have given you peace," she told me. "Your mind was dangerously close to madness. I have drugged you a little, physically; so your emotions will not be strong for a while. It was necessary to save your sanity."

It was true that my mind felt-was drugged the word? My thoughts were clear enough, but I felt as if I were submerged in transparent but dark water. There was an odd sense of existing in a dream. I remembered Swinburne's lines:

> *Here, where the world is quiet,*
> *Here, where all trouble seems*
> *Dead winds' and spent waves' riot*
> *In doubtful dreams of dreams....*

"What is this place?" I asked.

Lhar bent toward me. "I do not know if I can explain. It is not quite clear to me. The robot knows. He is a reasoning machine. Wait...." She turned to the sphere. Its cilia fluttered in quick, complicated signals.

Lhar turned back to me. "Do you know much of the nature of Time? That it is curved, moves in a spiral...."

She went on to explain, but much of her explanation I did not understand. Yet I gathered enough to realize that this valley was not of Earth. Or, rather, it was not of the earth I knew.

"You have geological disturbances, I know. The strata are tumbled about, mixed one with another —"

I remembered what Fra Rafael had said about an earthquake, three months before. Lhar nodded toward me.

"But this was a time-slip. The space-time continuum is also subject to great strains and stresses. It buckled, and strata-Time-sectors-were thrust up to mingle with others. This valley belongs to another age, as do I and the machine, and also-the Other."

She told me what had happened....There had been no warning. One moment she had been in her own World, her own Time. The next, she was here, with her robot. And with the Other....

"I do not know the origin of the Other. I may have lived in either your future or your past. This valley, with its ruined stone structures, is probably part of your future. I had never heard of such a place before. The Other may be of the future also. Its shape I do not know...."

* * * * *

She told me more, much more. The Other, as she called it-giving the entity a thought-form that implied complete alienage-had a strangely chameleon-like method of feeding. It lived on life-force, as well as I could understand, draining the vital powers of a mammal vampirically.

And it assumed the shape of its prey as it fed. It was not possession, in the strict sense of the word. It was a sort of merging....

Humanity is inclined to invest all things with its own attributes, forgetting that outside the limitations of time and space and size, familiar laws of nature do not apply.

So, even now I do not know all that lay behind the terror in that Peruvian valley. This much I learned: the Other, like Lhar and her robot, had been cast adrift by a time-slip, and thus marooned here. There was no way for it to return to its normal Time-sector. It had created the fog-wall to protect itself from the direct rays of the sun, which threatened its existence.

Sitting there in the filigreed, silver twilight beside Lhar, I had a concept of teeming universes of space-time, of an immense spiral of lives and civilizations, races and cultures, covering an infinite cosmos. And yet-what had happened? Very little, in that inconceivable infinity. A rift in time, a dimensional slip-and a sector of land and three beings on it had been wrenched from their place in time and transported to *our* time-stratum.

A robot, a flower that was alive and intelligent-and feminine-and the Other....

"The native girls," I said. "What will happen to them?"

"They are no longer alive," Lhar told me. "They still move and breathe, but they are dead, sustained only by the life-force of the Other. I do not think it will harm me. Apparently it prefers other food."

"That's why you've stayed here?" I asked.

The shining velvety calyx swayed. "I shall die soon. For a little while I thought that I might manage to survive in this alien world, this alien time. Your blood has helped." The cool tentacle withdrew from my arm. "But I lived in a younger time, where space was filled with-with certain energizing vibratory principles.

"They have faded now almost to nothing, to what you call cosmic rays. And these are too weak to maintain my life. No, I must die. And then my poor robot will be alone." I sensed elfin amusement in that last thought. "It seems absurd to you that I should think affectionately of a machine. But in our world there is a rapport —a mental symbiosis-between robot and living beings."

There was a silence. After a while I said, "I'd better get out of here. Get help-to end the menace of the other...." What sort of help I did not know. Was the Other vulnerable?

Lhar caught my thought. "In its own shape it is vulnerable, but what that shape is I do not know. As for your escaping from this valley-you cannot. The fog will bring you back."

"I've got my compass." I glanced at it, saw that the needle was spinning at random.

Lhar said: "The Other has many powers. Whenever you go into the fog, you will always return here."

"How do you know all this?" I asked.

"My robot tells me. A machine can reason logically, better than a colloid brain."

I closed my eyes, trying to think. Surely it should not be difficult for me to retrace my steps, to find a path out of this valley. Yet I hesitated, feeling a strange impotence.

"Can't your robot guide me?" I persisted.

"He will not leave my side. Perhaps —" Lhar turned to the sphere, and the cilia fluttered excitedly. "No," she said, turning back to me. "Built into his mind is one rule-never to leave me. He cannot disobey that."

* * * * *

I couldn't ask Lhar to go with me. Somehow I sensed that the frigid cold of the surrounding mountains would destroy her swiftly. I said, "It must be possible for me to get out of here. I'm going to try, anyway."

"I will be waiting," she said, and did not move as I slipped out between two trunks of the banyan-like tree.

It was daylight and the silvery grayness overhead was palely luminous. I headed for the nearest rampart of fog.

Lhar was right. Each time I went into that cloudy fog barrier I was blinded. I crept forward step by step, glancing behind me at my footprints in the snow, trying to keep in a straight line. And presently I would find myself back in the valley....

I must have tried a dozen times before giving up. There were no landmarks in that all-concealing grayness, and only by sheerest chance would anyone blunder into this valley-unless hypnotically summoned, like the Indio girls.

I realized that I was trapped. Finally I went back to Lhar. She hadn't moved an inch since I had left, nor had the robot, apparently.

"Lhar," I said. "Lhar, can't you help me?"

The white flame of the flower was motionless, but the robot's cilia moved in quick signals. Lhar moved at last.

"Perhaps," her thought came. "Unless both induction and deduction fail, my robot has discovered a chance for you. The Other can control your mind through emotions. But I, too, have some power over your mind. If I give you strength, wall you with a psychic shield against intrusion, you may be able to face the Other. But you cannot destroy it unless it is in its normal shape. The Indio girls must be killed first...."

"Killed?" I felt a sense of horror at the thought of killing those poor simple native girls.

"They are not actually alive now. They are now a part of the Other. They can never be restored to their former life."

"How will-destroying them-help me?" I asked.

Again Lhar consulted the robot. "The Other will be driven from their bodies. It will then have no hiding-place and must resume its own form. Then it can be slain."

Lhar swayed and curtseyed away. "Come," she said. "It is in my mind that the Other must die. It is evil, ruthlessly selfish, which is the same thing. Until now I have not realized the solution to this evil being. But seeing into your thoughts has clarified my own. And my robot tells me that unless I aid you, the Other will continue ravening into your world. If that happens, the time-pattern will be broken....I do not quite understand, but my robot makes no mistakes. The Other must die...."

She was outside of the banyan now, the sphere gliding after her. I followed. The three of us moved swiftly across the blue moss, guided by the robot.

In a little while we came to where the six Indio girls were squatting. They had apparently not moved since I had left them.

"The Other is not here," Lhar said.

The robot held me back as Lhar advanced toward the girls, the skirt-like frill at her base convoluting as she moved. She paused beside them and her petals trembled and began to unfold.

From the tip of that great blossom a fountain of white dust spurted up. Spores or pollen, it seemed to be. The air was cloudy with the whiteness.

The robot drew me back, back again. I sensed danger....

The pollen seemed to be drawn toward the Indios, spun toward them in dancing mist-motes. It settled on their bronzed bodies, their limbs and faces. It covered them like a veil until they appeared to be six statues, white as cold marble, there on the blue moss.

Lhar's petals lifted and closed again. She swayed toward me, her mind sending a message into mine.

"The Other has no refuge now," she told me. "I have slain the-the girls."

"They're dead?" My lips were dry.

"What semblance of life they had left is now gone. The Other cannot use them again."

Lhar swayed toward me. A cool tentacle swept out, pressing lightly on my forehead. Another touched my breast, above the heart.

"I give you of my strength," Lhar said. "It will be as shield and buckler to you. The rest of the way you must go alone...."

Into me tide of power flowed. I sank into cool depths, passionless and calm. Something was entering my body, my mind and soul, drowning my fears, stiffening my resolve.

51

Strength of Lhar was now my strength!

The tentacles dropped away, their work done. The robot's cilia signalled and Lhar said, "Your way lies there. That temple-do you see it?"

I saw it. Far in the distance, half shrouded by the fog, a scarlet structure, not ruined like the others, was visible.

"You will find the Other there. Slay the last Indio, then destroy the Other."

I had no doubt now of my ability to do that. A new power seemed to lift me from my feet, send me running across the moss. Once I glanced back, to see Lhar and her robot standing motionless, watching me.

The temple enlarged as I came nearer. It was built of the same reddish stone as the other ruined blocks I had seen. But erosion had weathered its harsh angles till nothing now remained but a rounded, smoothly sculptured monolith, twenty feet tall, shaped like a rifle shell.

A doorway gaped in the crimson wall. I paused for a moment on the threshold. In the dimness within a shadow stirred. I stepped forward, finding myself in a room that was tall and narrow, the ceiling hidden in gloom. Along the walls were carvings I could not clearly see. They gave a suggestion of inhuman beings that watched.

It was dark but I could see the Indio girl who had been Miranda Valle. Her eyes were on me, and, even through the protecting armor of Lhar strength; I could feel their terrible power.

The life in the girl was certainly not human!

"Destroy her!" my mind warned. "Destroy her! Quickly!"

But as I hesitated a veil of darkness seemed to fall upon me. Utter cold, a frigidity as of outer space, lanced into my brain. My senses reeled under the assault. Desperately, blind and sick and giddy, I called on the reserve strength Lhar had given me. Then I blacked out....

When I awoke I saw smoke coiling up from the muzzle of the pistol in my hand. At my feet lay the Indio girl, dead. My bullet had crashed into her brain, driving out the terrible dweller there.

My eyes were drawn to the farther wall. An archway gaped there. I walked across the room, passed under the archway. Instantly I was in complete, stygian darkness. But I was not alone!

The power of the Other struck me like a tangible blow. I have no words to tell of an experience so completely disassociated from human memories. I remember only this: my mind and soul were sucked down into a black abyss where I had no volition or consciousness. It was another dimension of the mind where my senses were altered....

Nothing existed there but the intense blackness beyond time and space. I could not see the Other nor conceive of it. It was pure intelligence, stripped of flesh. It was alive and it had power-power that was god-like.

There in the great darkness I stood alone, unaided, sensing the approach of an entity from some horribly remote place where all values were altered.

I sensed Lhar's nearness. "Hurry!" her thought came to me. "Before it wakens!"

Warmth flowed into me. The blackness receded....

Against the farther wall something lay, a thing bafflingly human ...a great-headed thing with a tiny pallid body coiled beneath it. It was squirming toward me....

"Destroy it!" Lhar communicated.

The pistol in my hand thundered, bucking against my palm. Echoes roared against the walls. I fired and fired again until the gun was empty....

"It is dead," Lhar's thought entered my mind.

I stumbled, dropped the pistol.

"It was the child of an old super-race —a child not yet born."

Can you conceive of such a race? Where even the unborn had power beyond human understanding? My mind wondered what the adult Alien must be.

I shivered, suddenly cold. An icy wind gusted through the temple. Lhar's thought was clear in my mind.

"Now the valley is no longer a barrier to the elements. The Other created fog and warmth to protect itself. Now it is dead and your world reclaims its own."

From the outer door of the temple I could see the fog being driven away by a swift wind. Snow was falling slowly, great white flakes that blanketed the blue moss and lay like caps on the red shards that dotted the valley.

"I shall die swiftly and easily now, instead of slowly, by starvation," Lhar said.

A moment later a thought crossed my mind, faint and intangible as a snowflake and I knew Lhar was saying goodbye.

I left the valley. Once I looked back, but there was only a veil of snow behind me.

And out of the greatest adventure the cosmic gods ever conceived-only this: For a little while the eternal veil of time was ripped away and the door to the unknown was held ajar.

But now the door is closed once more. Below Huascan a robot guards a tomb, that is all.

The snow fell faster. Shivering, I ploughed through the deepening drifts. My compass needle pointed north. The spell that had enthralled the valley was gone.

Half an hour later I found the trail, and the road to safety lay open before me. Fra Rafael would be waiting to hear my story.

But I did not think that he would believe it....

I, the Vampire

CHAPTER I
CHEVALIER FUTAINE

The party was dull. I had come too early. There was a preview that night at Grauman's Chinese, and few of the important guests would arrive until it was over. Jack Hardy, ace director at Summit Pictures, where I worked as assistant director, hadn't arrived-yet-and he was the host. But Hardy had never been noted for punctuality.

I went out on the porch and leaned against a coctail and looking down at the lights of Hollywood. Hardy's place was on the summit of a hill overlooking the film capital, near Falcon Lair, Valentino's famous turreted castle. I shivered a little. Fog was sweeping in from Santa Monica, blotting out the lights to the west.

Jean Hubbard, who was an ingenue at Summit, came up beside me and took the glass out of my hand.

"Hello, Mart," she said, sipping the liquor. "Where've you been?"

"Down with the Murder Desert troupe, on location in the Mojave," I said. "Miss me, honey?" I drew her close.

She smiled up at me, her tilted eyebrows lending a touch of diablerie to the tanned, lovely face. I was going to marry Jean, but I wasn't sure just when.

"Missed you lots," she said, and held up her lips. I responded.

After a moment I said, "What's this about the vampire man?"

She chuckled. "Oh, the Chevalier Futaine. Didn't you read Lolly Parsons', write-up in *Script*? Jack Hardy picked him up last month in Europe. Silly rot. Bill it's good publicity."

"Three cheers for publicity," I said. "Look what it did for *Birth of a Nation*. But where does the vampire angle come in?"

"Mystery man. Nobody can take a picture of him, scarcely anybody can meet him. Weird tales are told about his former life in Paris. Going to play in *Jack , Red Thirst*. The kind of build-up Universal gave Karloff for *Frankenstein*. Our Chevalier Futaine" —she rolled out the words with amused relish —"is probably a singing waiter from a Paris cafe. I haven't seen him-but the deuce with him, anyway. Mart, I want you to do something for me. For Deming."

"Hess Deming?" I raised my eyebrows in astonishment. Hess Deming, Summit's biggest box-office star, whose wife, Sandra Colter, had died two day before. She, too, had been an actress, although never the great star her husband was. Hess loved her, I knew-and now I guessed what the trouble was. I said, "I noticed he was a bit wobbly."

"He'll kill himself," Jean said, looking worried. "I—I feel responsible for him somehow, Mart. After all, he gave me my start at Summit. And he's due for the DTs any time now."

"Well, I'll do what I can," I told her. "But that isn't a great deal. After all, getting tight is probably the best thing he could do. I know if I lost you, Jean —"

I stopped. I didn't like to think of it.

Jean nodded. "Sec what you can do for him, anyway. Losing Sandra that way was-pretty terrible."

"What way?" I asked. "I've been away, remember. I read something aboul it, but —"

"She just died," Jean said. "Pernicious anemia, they said. But Hess told me the doctor really didn't know what it was. She just seemed to grow weaker and weaker until-she passed away."

I nodded, gave Jean a hasty kiss, and went back into the house. I had just seen Hess Deming walk past, a glass in his hand. He turned as I tapped his shoulder.

"Oh, Mart," he said, his voice just a bit fuzzy. He could hold his liquor, but I could tell by his bloodshot eyes that he was almost at the end of his rope. He was a handsome devil, all right, well-built, strong-featured, with level gray eyes and a broad mouth that was usually smiling. It wasn't smiling now. It was slack, and his face was bedewed with perspiration.

"You know about Sandra?" he asked.

"Yeah," I said. "I'm sorry, Hess."

He drank deeply from the glass, wiped his mouth with a grimace of distaste. "I'm drunk, Mart," he confided. "I had to get drunk. It was awful-those last few days. I've got to burn her up."

I didn't say anything.

"Burn her up. Oh, my God, Mart-that beautiful body of hers, crumbling to • In i -and I've got to watch it! She made me promise I'd watch to make sure they burned her."

I said, "Cremation's a clean ending, Hess. And Sandra was a clean girl, and a damned good actress."

He put his flushed face close to mine. "Yeah-but I've got to burn her up. It'll kill me, Mart. Oh, God!" He put the empty glass down on a table and looked around dazedly.

I was wondering why Sandra had insisted on cremation. She'd given an interview once in which she stressed her dread of fire. Most write-ups of stars are applesauce, but I happened to know that Sandra did dread fire. Once, on the set, I'd seen her go into hysterics when her leading man lit his pipe too near her face.

"Excuse me, Mart," Hess said. "I've got to get another drink."

"Wait a minute," I said, holding him. "You want to watch yourself, Hess, you've had too much already."

"It still hurts," he said. "Just a little more and maybe it won't hurt so much." But he didn't pull away. Instead he stared at me with the dullness of intoxication in his eyes. "Clean," he said presently.

"She said that too. Mart. She said burning was a clean death. But, God, that beautiful white body of hers —I can't stand it, Mart! I'm going crazy, I think. Get me a drink, like a good fellow."

I said, "Wait here, Hess. I'll get you one." I didn't add that it would be watered-considerably.

He sank down in a chair, mumbling thanks. As I went off I felt sick. I'd seen too many actors going on the rocks to mistake Hess's symptoms. I knew that his box office days were over. There would be longer and longer waits between features, and then personal appearances, and finally Poverty Row and serials. And in the end maybe a man found dead in a cheap hall bedroom on Main Street, with the gas on.

There was a crowd around the bar. Somebody said, "Here's Mart. Hey, come on and meet the vampire."

Then I got a shock. I saw Jack Hardy, my host, the director with whom I'd on many a hit. He looked like a corpse. And I'd seen him looking plenty Ixitl before. A man with a hangover or a marijuana jag isn't a pretty sight, but I'd never seen Hardy like this. He looked as though he was keeping going on his nerve alone. There was no blood in the man.

I'd last seen him as a stocky, ruddy blond, who looked like nothing so much as a wrestler, with his huge biceps, his ugly, good-natured face, and his bristling crop of yellow hair. Now he looked like a skeleton, with skin hanging loosely on the big frame. His face was a network of sagging wrinkles. Pouches bagged beneath his eyes, and those eyes were dull and glazed. About his neck a black silk scarf was knotted tightly.

"Good God, Jack!" I exclaimed. "What have you done to yourself?"

He looked away quickly. "Nothing," he said brusquely. "I'm all right. I want you to meet the Chevalier Futaine-this is Mart Prescott."

"Pierre," a voice said. "Hollywood is no place for titles. Mart Prescott-the pleasure is mine." I faced the Chevalier Pierre Futaine.

We shook hands. My first impression was of icy cold, and a slick kind of dryness-and I let go of his hand too quickly to be polite. He smiled at me.

A charming man, the chevalier. Or so he seemed. Slender, below medium height, his bland, round face seemed incongruously youthful. Blond hair was plastered close to his scalp. I saw that his cheeks were rouged-very deftly, but I know something about makeup. And under the rouge I read a curious, deathly pallor that would have made him a marked man had he not disguised it. Some disease, perhaps, had blanched his skin-but his lips were not artificially reddened. And they were as crimson as blood.

He was clean-shaved, wore impeccable evening clothes, and his eyes were black pools of ink. "Glad to know you," I said. "You're the vampire, eh?"

He smiled. "So they tell me. But we all serve the dark god of publicity, eh Mr. Prescott? Or-is it Mart?"

"It's Mart," I said, still staring at him. I saw his eyes go past me, and an extraordinary expression appeared on his face-an expression of amazement, disbelief. Swiftly it was gone.

I turned. Jean was approaching, was at my side as I moved. She said, "Is this the chevalier?"

Pierre Futaine was staring at her, his lips parted a little. Almost inaudibly he murmured, "Sonya." And then, on a note of interrogation, "Sonya?"

I introduced the two. Jean said, "You see, my name isn't Sonya."

The chevalier shook his head, an odd look in his black eyes.

"I once knew a girl like you," he said softly. "Very much like you. It's strange."

"Will you excuse me?" I broke in. Jack Hardy was leaving the bar. Quickly I followed him.

I touched his shoulder as he went out the French windows. He jerked out a snarled oath, turned a white death mask of a face to me.

"Damn you, Mart," he snarled. "Keep your hands to yourself."

I put my hands on his shoulders and swung him around.

"What the devil has happened to you?" I asked. "Listen, Jack, you can't bluff me or lie to me. You know that. I've straightened you out enough times in the past, and I can do it again. Let me in on it."

His ruined face softened. He reached up and took away my hands. His own were ice-cold, like the hands of the Chevalier Futaine.

"No," he said. "No use, Mart. There's nothing you can do. I'm all right, really. Just-over-strain. I had too good a time in Paris."

I was up against a blank wall. Suddenly, without volition, a thought popped into my mind and out of my mouth before I knew it.

"What's the matter with your neck?" I asked abruptly.

He didn't answer. He just frowned and shook his head.

"I've a throat infection," he told me. "Caught it on the steamer."

His hand went up and touched the black scarf.

There was a croaking, harsh sound from behind us —a sound that didn't seem quite human. I turned. It was Hess Deming. He was swaying in the portal, his eyes glaring and bloodshot, a little trickle of saliva running down his chin.

He said in a dead, expressionless voice that was somehow dreadful, "Sandra died of a throat infection, Hardy."

Jack didn't answer. He stumbled back a step. Hess went on dully.

"She got all white and died. And the doctor didn't know what it was, although the death certificate said anemia. Did you bring back some filthy disease with you, Hardy? Because if you did I'm going to kill you."

"Wait a minute," I said. "A throat infection? I didn't know —"

"There was a wound on her throat-two little marks, close together. That wouldn't have killed her, unless some loathsome disease —"

"You're crazy, Hess," I said. "You know you're drunk. Listen to me: Jack couldn't have had anything to do with-that."

Hess didn't look at me. He watched Jack Hardy out of his bloodshot eyes. He went on in that low, deadly monotone:

"Will you swear Mart's right, Hardy? Will you?"

Jack's lips were twisted by some inner agony. I said, "Go on, Jack. Tell him he's wrong."

Hardy burst out, "I haven't been near your wife! I haven't seen her since I got back. There's —
"

"That's not the answer I want," Hess whispered. And he sprang for the other IIMII reeled forward, rather.

Hess was too drunk, and Jack too weak, for them to do each other any harm, but there was a nasty scuffle for a moment before I separated them. As I pulled them apart, Hess's hand clutched the scarf about Jack's neck, ripped it away.

And I saw the marks on Jack Hardy's throat. Two red, angry little pits, white rimmed, just over the Iclt jugular.

CHAPTER II
THE CREMATION OF SANDRA

It was the next day that Jean telephoned me.

"Mart," she said, "we're going to run over a scene for *Red Thirst* tonight at the studio-Stage 6. You've been assigned as assistant director for the pic, so you should be there. And—I had an idea Jack might not tell you. He's been-so odd lately."

"Thanks, honey," I said. "I'll be there. But I didn't know you were in the flicker."

"Neither did I, but there's been some wire-pulling. Somebody wanted me in it-the chevalier, I think-and the big boss phoned me this morning and let me in on the secret. I don't feel up to it, though. Had a bad night."

"Sorry," I sympathized. "You were okay when I left you."

"I had a—nightmare," she said slowly. "It was rather frightful, Mart. It's funny, though, I can't remember what it was about. Well-you'll be there tonight?"

I said I would, but as it happened I was unable to keep my promise. Hess Deming telephoned me, asking if I'd come out to his Malibu place and drive him into town. He was too shaky to handle a car himself, he said, and Sandra's cremation was to take place that afternoon. I got out my roadster and sent it spinning west on Sunset. In twenty minutes I was at Deming's beach house The houseboy let me in, shaking his head gravely as he recognized me. "Mist' Doming pretty bad," he told me. "All morning drinking gin straight—"

From upstairs Hess shouted, "That you, Mart? Okay—I'll be down right away. Come up here, Jim!"

The Japanese, with a meaningful glance at me, pattered upstairs.

I wandered over to a table, examining the magazines upon it. A little breeze of wind came through the half-open window, fluttering a scrap of paper. A word on it caught my eye, and I picked up the note. For that's what it was. It was addressed to Hess, and after one glance I had no compunction about scanning it. "Hess dear," the message read. "I feel I'm going to die very soon. And I want you to do something for me. I've been out of my head, I know, saying things I didn't mean. Don't cremate me, Hess. Even though I were dead I'd feel the fire—I know it. Bury me in a vault in Forest Lawn-and don't embalm me. I shall be dead when you find this, but I know you'll do as I wish, dear. And alive or dead, I'll always love you."

The note was signed by Sandra Colter, Hess's wife. This was (Kid. I wondered whether Hess had seen it yet.

There was a little hiss of indrawn breath from behind me. It was Jim, the houseboy. He said, "Mist' Prescott, I find that note last night. Mist' Hess not seen it. It Mis' Colter's writing."

He hesitated, and I read fear in his eyes-sheer, unashamed fear. He put a brown forefinger on the note.

"See that, Mist' Prescott?"

He was pointing to a smudge of ink that half obscured the signature. I said, "Well?"

"I do that, Mist' Prescott. When I pick up the note. The ink-not dry."

I stared at him. He turned hastily at the sound of footsteps on the stairs. Hess Deming was coming down, rather shakily.

I think it was then that I first realized the horrible truth. I didn't believe it, though-not then. It was too fantastic, too incredible; yet something of the truth must have crept into my mind, for there was no other explanation for what I did then.

Hess said, "What have you got there, Mart?"

"Nothing," I said quietly. I crumpled the note and thrust it into my pocket. "Nothing important, anyway. Ready to go?"

He nodded, and we went to the door. I caught a glimpse of Jim staring after us, an expression of-was it relief? —in his dark, wizened face.

The crematory was in Pasadena, and I left Hess there. I would have stayed with him, but he wouldn't have it. I knew he didn't want anyone to be watching him when Sandra's body was being incinerated. And I knew it would be easier for him that way. I took a short cut through the Hollywood hills, and that's where the trouble started.

I broke an axle. Recent rains had gullied the road, and I barely saved the car from turning over. After that I had to hike miles to the nearest telephone, and then I wasted more time waiting for a taxi to pick me up. It was nearly eight o'clock when I arrived at the studio.

The gateman let me in, and I hurried to Stage 6. It was dark. Cursing under my breath, I turned away, and almost collided with a small figure. It was Forrest, one of the cameramen. He let out a curious squeal, and clutched my arm.

"That you, Mart? Listen, will you do me a favor? I want you to watch a I uint —"

"Haven't time," I said. "Seen Jean around here? I was to —"

"It's about that," Forrest said. He was a shriveled, monkey-faced little chap, but a mighty good cameraman. "They've gone-Jean and Hardy and the chevalier. There's something funny about that guy."

"Think so? Well, I'll phone Jean. I'll look at your rushes tomorrow."

"She won't be home," he told me. "The chevalier took her over to the 1 uovc Listen, Mart, you've got to watch this. Either I don't know how to handle i runder any more, or that Frenchman is the damnedest thing I've ever shot, come over to the theater. Mart I've got the reel ready to run. Just developed the rough print myself."

"Oh, all right," I assented, and followed Forrest to the theater.

I found a seat in the dark little auditorium, and listened to Forrest moving about in the projection booth. He clicked on the amplifier and said: "Hardy didn't warn any pictures taken-insisted on it, you know. But the boss told me to leave one of the automatic cameras going-not to bother with the sound-just to get an idea how the French guy would screen. Lucky it wasn't one of the old rattler cameras, or Hardy would have caught on. Here it comes, Mart!"

I heard a click as the amplifier was switched off. White light flared on the screen. It faded, gave place to a picture-the interior of Stage 6. The set was incongruous —a mid-Victorian parlor, with overstuffed plush chairs, gilt-edged paintings, even a particularly hideous what-not. Jack Hardy moved into the range of the camera. On the screen his face seemed to leap out at me like a death's-head, covered with sagging, wrinkled skin. Following him came Jean, wearing a tailored suit-no one dresses for rehearsals-and behind her —

I blinked, thinking that my eyes were tricking me. Something like a glowing fog-oval, tall as a man-was moving across the screen. You've seen the nimbus of light on the screen when a flashlight is turned directly on the camera? Well-it was like that, except that its source was not traceable. And, horribly, it moved forward at about the pace a man would walk.

The amplifier clicked again. Forrest said, "When I saw it on the negative I thought I was screwy, Mart. I saw the take-there wasn't any funny light there —"

The oval, glowing haze was motionless beside Jean, and she was looking directly at it, a smile on her lips. "Mart, when that was taken, Jean was looking right at the French guy!"

I said, somewhat hoarsely, "Hold it, Forrest. Right there."

The images slowed down, became motionless. Jean's profile was toward the camera. I leaned forward, staring at something I had glimpsed on the girl's neck. It was scarcely visible save as a tiny, discolored mark on Jean's throat, above the jugular-but unmistakably the same wound I had seen on the throat of Jack Hardy the night before!

I heard the amplifier click off. Suddenly the screen showed blindingly white, and then went black.

I waited a moment, but there was no sound from the booth.

"Forrest," I called. "You okay?"

There was no sound. The faint whirring of the projector had died. I got up quickly and went to the back of the theater. There were two entrances to the booth, a door which opened on stairs leading down to the alley outside, and a hole in the floor reached by means of a metal ladder. I went up this swiftly, an ominous apprehension mounting within me.

Forrest was still there. But he was no longer alive. He lay sprawled on his back, his wizened face staring up blindly, his head twisted at an impossible angle. It was quite apparent that his neck had been broken almost instantly.

I sent a hasty glance at the projector. The can of film was gone! And the door opening on the stairway was ajar a few inches.

I stepped out on the stairs, although I knew I would see no one. The white-lit broad alley between Stages 6 and 4 was silent and empty.

The sound of running feet came to me, steadily growing louder. A man came racing into view. I recognized him as one of the publicity gang. I hailed him.

"Can't wait," he gasped, but slowed down nevertheless.

I said, "Have you seen anyone around here just now? The-Chevalier Futaine?"

He shook his head. "No, but —" His face was white as he looked up at me. "Hess Deming's gone crazy. I've got to contact the papers."

Ice gripped me. I raced down the stairs, clutched his arm.

"What do you mean?" I snapped. "Hess was all right when I left him. A bit tight, that's all."

His face was glistening with sweat. "It's awful —I'm not sure yet what happened. His wife-Sandra Colter-came to life while they were cremating her. They saw her through the window, you know-screaming and pounding at the glass while she was being burned alive. Hess got her out too late. He went stark, raving mad. Suspended animation, they say —I've got to get to a phone, Mr. Prescott!"

He tore himself away, sprinted in the direction of the administration buildings.

I put my hand in my pocket and pulled out a scrap of paper. It was the note I had found in Hess Deming's house. The words danced and wavered before my eyes. Over and over I was telling myself, "It can't be true! Such things can't happen!"

I didn't mean Sandra Colter's terrible resurrection during the cremation. That, alone, might be plausibly explained-catalepsy, perhaps. But taken in conjunction with certain other occurrences, it led to one definite conclusion-and it was a conclusion I dared not face.

What had poor Forrest said? That the chevalier was taking Jean to the Cocoanut Grove? Well —

The taxi was still waiting. I got in.

"The Ambassador," I told the driver grimly. "Twenty bucks if you hit the green lights all the way."

CHAPTER III
THE BLACK COFFIN

All night I had been combing Hollywood-without success. Neither the Chevalier Futaine nor Jean had been to the Grove, I discovered. And no one knew the Chevalier's address. A telephone call to the studio, now ablaze with the excitement over the Hess Dcming disaster and the Forrest killing, netted me exactly nothing. I went the rounds of Hollywood night life vainly. The Trocadero, Sardi's, all three of the Brown Derbies, the smart, notorious clubs of the Sunset eighties-nowhere could I find my quarry. I telephoned Jack Hardy a dozen times, but got no answer. Finally, in a "private club" in Culver City, I met with my first stroke of good luck.

"Mr. Hardy's upstairs," the proprietor told me, looking anxious. "Nothin' wrong, I hope, Mr. Prescott? I heard about Deming."

"Nothing," I said. "Take me up to him."

"He's sleeping it off," the man admitted. "Tried to drink the place dry, and I put him upstairs where he'd be safe."

"Not the first time, eh?" I said, with an assumption of lightness. "Well, bring up some coffee, will you? Black. I've got to-talk to him."

But it was half an hour before Hardy was in any shape to understand what I was saying. At last he sat up on the couch, blinking, and a gleam of realization came into his sunken eyes.

"Prescott," he said, "can't you leave me alone?"

I leaned close to him, articulating carefully so he would be sure to understand me. "I know what the Chevalier Futaine is," I said.

And I waited for the dreadful, impossible confirmation, or for the words which would convince me that I was an insane fool.

Hardy looked at me dully. "How did you find out?" he whispered.

An icy shock went through me. Up to that moment I had not really believed, in spite of all the evidence. But now Hardy was confirming the suspicions which I had not let myself believe.

I didn't answer his question. Instead, I said, "Do you know about Hess?" He nodded, and at sight of the agony in his face I almost pitied him. Then the thought of Jean steadied me.

"Do you know where he is now?" I asked.

"No. What are you talking about?" he flared suddenly. "Are you mad, Mart? Do you —"

"I'm not mad. But Hess Deming is."

He looked at me like a cowering, whipped dog.

I went on grimly: "Are you going to tell me the truth? How you got those marks on your throat? How you met this-creature? And where he's taken Jean?"

"Jean!" He looked genuinely startled. "Has he got—I didn't know that, Mart—I swear I didn't. You-you've been a good friend to me, and-and I'll tell you the truth-for your sake and Jean's —although now it may be too late." My involuntary movement made him glance at me quickly. Then he went on. "I met him in Paris. I was out after new sensations-but I didn't expect anything like that. A Satanist club-devil-worshippers, they were. The ordinary stuff-cheap, furtive blasphemy. But it was there that I met-him.

"He can be a fascinating chap when he tries. He drew me out, made me tell him about Hollywood-about the women we have here. I bragged a little. He asked me about the stars, whether they were really as beautiful as they seemed. His eyes were hungry as he listened to me, Mart.

"Then one night I had a fearful nightmare. A monstrous, black horror crept in through the window and attacked me-bit me in the throat, I dreamed, or thought I did. After that —

"I was in his power. He told me the truth. He made me his slave, and I could do nothing. His powers-are not human."

I licked dry lips.

Hardy continued: "He made me bring him here, introducing him as a new discovery to be starred in *Red Thirst* —I'd mentioned the picture to him, before I —knew. How he must have laughed at me! He made me serve him, keeping away photographers, making sure that there were no cameras, no mirrors near him. And for a reward-he let me live."

I knew I should feel contempt for Hardy, panderer to such a loathsome evil. But somehow I couldn't.

I said quietly, "What about Jean? Where does the chevalier live?"

He told me. "But you can't do anything, Mart. There's a vault under the house, where he stays during the day. It can't be opened, except with a key he always keeps with him —a silver key. He had a door specially made, and then did something to it so that nothing can open it but that key. Even dynamite wouldn't do it, he told me."

I said, "Such things-can be killed."

"Not easily. Sandra Colter was a victim of his. After death she, too, became a vampire, sleeping by day and living only at night. The fire destroyed her, but there's no way to get into the vault under Futaine's house."

"I wasn't thinking of fire," I said. "A knife —"

"Through the heart," Hardy interrupted almost eagerly. "Yes-and decapitation. I've thought of it myself, but I can do nothing. I —am his slave, Mart."

I said nothing, but pressed the bell. Presently the proprietor appeared.

"Can you get me a butcher knife?" I measured with my hands. "About so long? A sharp one?"

Accustomed to strange requests, he nodded. "Right away, Mr. Prescott." As I followed him out, Hardy said weakly, "Mart."

I turned.

"Good luck," he said. The look on his wrecked face robbed the words of their pathos.

"Thanks," I forced myself to say. "I don't blame you, Jack, for what's happened. I —I'd have done the same."

I left him there, slumped on the couch, staring after me with eyes that had looked into hell.

It was past daylight when I drove out of Culver City, a long, razor-edged knife hidden securely inside my coat. And the day went past all too quickly. A telephone call told me that Jean had not yet returned home. It took me more than an hour to locate a certain man I wanted —a man who had worked for the studio before on certain delicate jobs. There was little about locks he did not know, as the Police had sometimes ruefully admitted.

His name was Axel Ferguson, a bulky, good-natured Swede, whose thick fingers seemed more adapted to handling a shovel than the mcchanisms of locks. Yet he was as expert as Houdini-indeed, he had at one time been a professional magician.

The front door of Futaine's isolated canyon home proved no bar to Ferguson's fingers and the tiny sliver of steel he used. The house, a modern two-story place, seemed deserted. But Hardy had said below the house.

We went down the cellar stairs and found ourselves in a concrete-lined passage that ran down at a slight angle for perhaps thirty feet. There the corridor ended in what seemed to be a blank wall of bluish steel. The glossy surface of the door was unbroken, save for a single keyhole.

Ferguson set to work. At first he hummed under his breath, but after a time he worked in silence. Sweat began to glisten on his face. Trepidation assailed me as I watched.

The flashlight he had placed beside him grew dim. He inserted another battery, got out unfamiliar-looking apparatus. He buckled on dark goggles, and handed me a pair. A blue, intensely brilliant flame began to play on the door. It was useless. The torch was discarded after a time, and Ferguson returned to his tools. He was using a stethoscope, taking infinite pains in the delicate movements of his hands.

It was fascinating to watch him. But all the time I realized that the night was coming, that presently the sun would go down, and that the life of the vampire lasts from sunset to sunrise.

At last Ferguson gave up. "I can't do it," he told me, panting as though from a hard race. "And if I can't, nobody can. Even Houdini couldn't have broken this lock. The only thing that'll open it is the key."

"All right, Axel," I said dully. "Here's your money."

He hesitated, watching me. "You going to stay here. Mr. Prescott?"

"Yeah," I said. "You can find your way out. I'll-wait awhile."

"Well, I'll leave the light with you," he said. "You can let me have it sometime, eh?"

He waited, and, as I made no answer, he departed, shaking his head.

Then utter silence closed around me. I took the knife out of my coat, tested its edge against my thumb, and settled back to wait.

Less than half an hour later the steel door began to swing open. I stood up. Through the widening crack I saw a bare, steel-lined chamber, empty save for a long, black object that rested on the floor. It was a coffin.

The door was wide. Into view moved a white, slender figure-Jean, clad in a diaphanous, silken robe. Her eyes were wide, fixed and staring. She looked like a sleepwalker.

A man followed her —a man wearing impeccable evening clothes. Not a hair was out of place on his sleek blond head, and he was touching his lips delicately with a handkerchief as he came out of the vault.

There was a little crimson stain on the white linen where his lips had brushed

CHAPTER IV
I, THE VAMPIRE

Jean walked past me as though I didn't exist. But the Chevalier Futaine paused, his eyebrows lifted. His black eyes pierced through me.

The handle of the knife was hot in my hand. I moved aside to block Futaine's way. Behind me came a rustle of silk, and from the corner of my eye I saw Jean pause hesitatingly.

The chevalier eyed me, toying negligently with his handkerchief. "Mart," he said slowly. "Mart Prescott." His eyes flickered toward the knife, and a little smile touched his lips.

I said, "You know why I'm here, don't you?"

"Yes," he said. "I—heard you. I was not disturbed. Only one thing can open this door." From his pocket he drew a key, shining with a dull silver sheen.

"Only this," he finished, replacing it. "Your knife is useless, Mart Prescott."

"Maybe," I said, edging forward very slightly. "What have you done to Jean?"

A curious expression, almost of pain, flashed into his eyes. "She is mine," he shot out half angrily. "You can do nothing, for—"

I sprang then, or, at least, I tried to. The blade of the knife sheared down straight for Futaine's white shirtfront. It was arrested in midair. Yet he had not moved. His eyes had bored into mine, suddenly, terribly, and it seemed as though a wave of fearful energy had blasted out at me-paralyzing me, rendering me helpless. I stood rigid. Veins throbbed in my temples as I tried to move-to bring down the knife. It was useless. I stood as immovable as a statue.

The chevalier brushed past me.

"Follow," he said almost casually, and like an automaton I swung about, began to move along the passage. What hellish hypnotic power was this that held me helpless?

Futaine led the way upstairs. It was not yet dark, although the sun had gone down. I followed him into a room, and at his gesture dropped into a chair. At my side was a small table. The chevalier touched my arm gently, and something like a mild electric shock went through me. The knife dropped from my fingers, clattering to the table.

Jean was standing rigidly nearby, her eyes dull and expressionless. Futaine moved to her side, put an arm about her waist. My mouth felt as though it were filled with mud, but somehow I managed to croak out articulate words.

"Damn you, Futaine! Leave her alone!"

He released her, and came toward me, his face dark with anger.

"You fool, I could kill you now, very easily. I could make you go down to the busiest corner of Hollywood and slit your throat with that knife. I have the—"

The face of a beast looking into mine. He snarled. "She is not yours. Nor is she-Jean. She is Sonya."

I remembered what Futaine had murmured when he had first seen Jean. He read the question in my eyes.

"I knew a girl like that once, very long ago. That was Sonya. They killed her-put a stake through her heart, long ago in Thurn. Now that I've found this girl, who might be a reincarnation of Sonya-they are so alike —I shall not give her up. Nor can anyone force me."

"You've made her a devil like yourself," I said through half-paralyzed lips. "I'd rather kill her—"

Futaine turned to watch Jean. "Not yet," he said softly. "She is mine-yes. She bears the stigmata. But she is still-alive. She will not become —*wampyr* until she has died, or until she has tasted the red milk. She shall do that tonight." I cursed him bitterly, foully. He touched my lips, and I could utter no sound. Then they left me-Jean and her master. I heard a door close quietly.

The night dragged on. Futile struggles had convinced me that it was useless to attempt escape —I could not even force a whisper through my lips. More than once I felt myself on the verge of madness-thinking of Jean, and remembering Futaine's ominous words. Eventually agony brought its own surcease, and I fell into a kind of coma, lasting for how long I could not guess. Many hours had passed, I knew, before I heard footsteps coming toward my prison.

Jean moved into my range of vision. I searched her face with my eyes, seeking for some mark of a dreadful metamorphosis. I could find none. Her beauty was unmarred, save for the terrible little wounds on her throat. She went to a couch and quietly lay down. Her eyes closed.

The chevalier came past me and went to Jean's side. He stood looking down at her. I have mentioned before the incongruous youthfulness of his face. That was gone now. He looked old—old beyond imagination.

At last he shrugged and turned to me. His fingers brushed my lips again, and I found that I could speak. Life flooded back into my veins, benign lancing twinges of pain. I moved an arm experimentally. The paralysis was leaving me. The chevalier said, "She is still-clean. I could not do it."

Amazement flooded me. My eyes widened in disbelief.

Futaine smiled wryly. "It is quite true. I could have made her as myself-undead. But at the last moment I forbade her." He looked toward the windows. "It will be dawn soon."

I glanced at the knife on the table beside me. The chevalier put out a hand and drew it away. "Wait," he said. "There is something I must tell you, Mart Prescott. You say that you know who and what I am."

I nodded.

"Through the ages I have come, since first I fell victim to another vampire-for thus is the evil spread. Deathless and not alive, bringing fear and sorrow always, knowing the bitter agony of Tantalus, I have gone down through the weary centuries. I have known Richard and Henry and Elizabeth of England, and ever have I brought terror and destruction in the night, for I am an alien thing, I am the undead."

The quiet voice went on, holding me motionless in its weird spell.

"I, the vampire. I, the accursed, the shining evil, *negotium perambulans in tenebris* . . . but I was not always thus. Long ago in Thurn, before the shadow leapt upon me, I loved a girl-Sonya. But the vampire visited me, and I sickened and died-and awoke. Then I arose.

"It is the curse of the undead to prey upon those they love. I visited Sonya.

"I made her my own. She, too, died, and for a brief while we walked the earth together, neither alive nor dead. But that was not Sonya. It was her body, yes, but I had not loved her body alone. I realized too late that I had destroyed her utterly."

"One day they opened her grave, and the priest drove a stake through her heart, and gave her rest. Me they could not find, for my coffin was hidden too well. I put love behind me then, knowing that there was none for such as I.

"Hope came to me when I found-Jean. Hundreds of years have passed since Sonya crumbled to dust, but I thought I had found her again. And—I took her. Nothing human could prevent me."

The chevalier's eyelids sagged. He looked infinitely old.

"Nothing human. Yet in the end I found that I could not condemn her to the It.'ll that is mine. I thought I had forgotten love. But, long and long ago, I loved Sonya. And, because of her, and because I know that I would only destroy, as I did once before, I shall not work my will on this girl."

I turned to watch the still figure on the couch. The chevalier followed my gaze and nodded slowly.

"Yes, she bears the stigmata. She will die, unless" —he met my gaze unblinkingly —"unless I die. If you had broken into the vault yesterday, if you had sunk that knife into my heart, she would be free now." He glanced at the windows again. "The sun will rise soon."

Then he went quickly to Jean's side. He looked down at her for a moment. "She is very beautiful," he murmured. "Too beautiful for hell."

The chevalier swung about, went toward the door. As he passed me he threw something carelessly on the table, something that tinkled as it fell. In the portal he paused, and a little smile twisted the scarlet lips. I remembered him thus, framed against the black background of the doorway, his sleek blond head erect and unafraid. He lifted his arm in a gesture that should have been theatrical, but, somehow, wasn't.

"And so farewell. I who am about to die —"

He did not finish. In the faint grayness of dawn I saw him striding away, heard his foot-steps on the stairs, receding and faint-heard a muffled clang as of a great door closing. The paralysis had left me. I was trembling a little, for I realized what I must do soon. But I knew I would not fail.

I glanced down at the table. Even before I saw what lay beside the knife, I knew what would be there. A silver key. . . .

The Salem Horror

When Carson first noticed the sounds in his cellar, he ascribed them to the rats. Later he began to hear the tales which were whispered by the superstitious Polish mill workers in Derby Street regarding the first occupant of the ancient house, Abigail Prinn. There was none living today who could remember the diabolical old hag, but the morbid legends which thrive in the "witch district" of Salem like rank weeds on a neglected grave gave disturbing particulars of her activities, and were unpleasantly explicit regarding the detestable sacrifices she was known to have made to a worm-eaten, crescent-horned image of dubious origin. The oldsters still muttered of Abbie Prinn and her monstrous boasts that she was high priestess of a fearfully potent god which dwelt deep in the hills. Indeed, it was the old witch's reckless boasting which had led to her abrupt and mysterious death in 1692, about the time of the famous hangings on Gallows Hill. No one liked to talk about it, but occasionally a toothless crone would mumble fearfully that the flames could not burn her, for her whole body had taken on the peculiar anesthesia of her witch-mark.

Abbie Prinn and her anomalous statue had long since vanished, but it was still difficult to find tenants for her decrepit, gabled house, with its overhanging second story and curious diamond-paned casement windows. The house's evil notoriety had spread throughout Salem. Nothing had actually happened there of recent years which might give rise to the inexplicable tales, but those who rented the house had a habit of moving out hastily, generally with vague and unsatisfactory explanations connected with the rats.

And it was a rat which led Carson to the Witch Room. The squealing and muffled pattering within the rotting walls had disturbed Carson more than once during the nights of his first week in the house, which he had rented to obtain the solitude that would enable him to complete a novel for which his publishers had been asking — another light romance to add to Carson's long string of popular successes. But it was not until sometime later that he began to entertain certain wildly fantastic surmises regarding the intelligence of the rat that scurried from under his feet in the dark hallway one evening.

The house had been wired for electricity, but the bulb in the hall was small and gave a dim light. The rat was a misshapen, black shadow as it darted a few feet away and paused, apparently watching him.

At another time Carson might have dismissed the animal with a threatening gesture and returned to his work. But the traffic on Derby Street had been unusually noisy, and he had found it difficult to concentrate upon his novel. His nerves, for no apparent reason, were taut; and somehow it seemed that the rat, watching just beyond his reach, was eyeing him with sardonic amusement.

Smiling at the conceit, he took a few steps toward the rat, and it rushed away to the cellar door, which he saw with surprise was ajar. He must have neglected to close it the last time he had been in the cellar, although he generally took care to keep the doors shut, for the ancient house was drafty. The rat waited in the doorway.

Unreasonably annoyed, Carson hurried forward, sending the rat scurrying down the stairway. He switched on the cellar light and observed the rat in a corner. It watched him keenly out of glittering little eyes.

As he descended the stairs he could not help feeling that he was acting like a fool. But his work had been tiring, and subconsciously he welcomed any interruption. He moved across the cellar to the rat, seeing with astonishment that the creature remained unmoving, staring at him. A strange feeling of uneasiness began to grow within him. The rat was acting abnormally, he felt; and the unwinking gaze of its cold shoe-button eyes was somehow disturbing.

Then he laughed to himself, for the rat had suddenly whisked aside and disappeared into a little hole in the cellar wall. Idly he scratched a cross with his toe in the dirt before the burrow, deciding that he would set a trap there in the morning.

The rat's snout and ragged whiskers protruded cautiously. It moved forward and then hesitated, drew back. Then the animal began to act in a singular and unaccountable manner-almost as though it were dancing, Carson thought. It moved tentatively forward, retreated again. It would give a little dart forward and be brought up short, then leap back hastily, as though-the simile flashed into Carson's mind —a snake were coiled before the burrow, alert to prevent the rat's escape. But there was nothing there save the little cross Carson had scratched in the dust.

No doubt it was Carson himself who blocked the rat's escape, for he was standing within a few feet of the burrow. He moved forward, and the animal hurriedly retreated out of sight.

His interest piqued, Carson found a stick and poked it exploringly into the hole. As he did so his eye, close to the wall, detected something strange about the stone slab just above the rat burrow. A quick glance around its edge confirmed his suspicion. The slab was apparently movable.

Carson examined it closely, noticed a depression on its edge which would afford a handhold. His fingers fitted easily into the groove, and he pulled tentatively. The stone moved a trifle and stopped. He pulled harder, and with a sprinkling of dry earth the slab swung away from the wall as though on hinges.

A black rectangle, shoulder-high, gaped in the wall. From its depths a musty, unpleasant stench of dead air welled out, and involuntarily Carson retreated a step. Suddenly he remembered the monstrous tales of Abbie Prinn and the hideous secrets she was supposed to have kept hidden in her house. Had he stumbled upon some hidden retreat of the long-dead witch?

Before entering the dark gap he took the precaution of obtaining a flashlight from upstairs. Then he cautiously bent his head and stepped into the narrow, evil-smelling passage, sending the flashlight's beam probing out before him.

He was in a narrow tunnel, scarcely higher than his head, and walled and paved with stone slabs. It ran straight ahead for perhaps fifteen feet, and then broadened out into a roomy chamber. As Carson stepped into the underground room-no doubt a hidden retreat of Abbie Prinn's, a hiding-place, he thought, which nevertheless could not save her on the day the fright-crazed mob had come raging along Derby Street-he caught "his breath in a gasp of amazement. The room was fantastic, astonishing.

It was the floor which held Carson's gaze. The dull gray of the circular wall gave place here to a mosaic of varicolored stone, in which blues and greens and purples predominated-indeed, there were none of the warmer colors. There must have been thousands of bits of colored stone making up that pattern, for none was larger than a walnut. And the mosaic seemed to follow some definite pattern, unfamiliar to Carson; there were curves of purple and violet mingled with angled lines of green and blue, intertwining in fantastic arabesques. There were circles, triangles, a pentagram, and other, less familiar, figures. Most of the lines and figures radiated from a definite point: the center of the chamber, where there was a circular disk of dead black stone perhaps two feet in diameter.

It was very silent. The sounds of the cars that occasionally went past overhead in Derby Street could not be heard. In a shallow alcove in the wall Carson caught a glimpse of markings on the walls, and he moved slowly in that direction, the beam of his light traveling up and down the walls of the niche.

The marks, whatever they were, had been daubed upon the stone long ago, for what was left of the cryptic symbols was indecipherable. Carson saw several partly effaced hieroglyphics which reminded him of Arabic, but he could not be sure. On the floor of the alcove was a corroded metal disk about eight feet in diameter, and Carson received the distinct impression that it was movable. But there seemed no way to lift it.

He became conscious that he was standing in the exact center of the chamber, in the circle of black stone where the odd design centered. Again he noticed the utter silence. On an impulse he clicked off the ray of his flashlight. Instantly he was in dead blackness.

At that moment a curious idea entered his mind. He pictured himself at the bottom of a pit, and from above a flood was descending, pouring down the shaft to engulf him. So strong was this impression that he actually fancied he could hear a muffled thundering, the roar of the cataract. Then, oddly shaken, he clicked on the light, glanced around swiftly. The drumming, of course, was the pounding of his blood, made audible in the complete silence —a familiar phenomenon. But, if the place was so still —

The thought leaped into his mind, as though suddenly thrust into his consciousness. This would be an ideal place to work. He could have the place wired for electricity, have a table and chair brought down, use an electric fan if necessary-although the musty odor he had first noticed seemed to have disappeared completely. He moved to the tunnel mouth, and as he stepped from the room he felt an inexplicable relaxation of his muscles, although he had not realized that they had been contracted. He ascribed it to nervousness, and went upstairs to brew black coffee and write to his landlord in Boston about his discovery.

The visitor stared curiously about the hallway after Carson had opened the door, nodding to himself as though with satisfaction. He was a lean, tll figure of a man, with thick steel-gray eyebrows overhanging keen gray eyes. His face, although strongly marked and gaunt, was unwrinkled.

"About the Witch Room, I suppose?" Carson said ungraciously. His landlord had talked, and for the last week he had been unwillingly entertaining antiquaries and occultists anxious to glimpse the secret chamber in which Abbie Prinn had mumbled her spells. Carson's annoyance had grown, and he had considered moving to a quieter place; but his inherent stubbornness had made him stay on, determined to finish his novel in spite of interruptions. Now, eyeing his guest coldly, he said, "I'm sorry, but it's not on exhibition anymore."

The other looked startled, but almost immediately a gleam of comprehension came into his eyes. He extracted a card and offered it to Carson.

"Michael Leigh . . . occultist, eh?" Carson repeated. He drew a deep breath. The occultists, he had found, were the worst, with their dark hints of nameless things and their profound interest in the mosaic pattern on the floor of the Witch Room. "I'm sorry, Mr. Leigh, but — I'm really quite busy. You'll excuse me."

Ungraciously he turned back to the door.

"Just a moment," Leigh said swiftly.

Before Carson could protest he had caught the writer by the shoulders and was peering closely into his eyes. Startled, Carson drew back, but not before he had seen an extraordinary expression of mingled apprehension and satisfaction appear on Leigh's gaunt face. It was as though the occultist had seen something unpleasant-but not unexpected.

"What's the idea?" Carson asked harshly. "I'm not accustomed —"

"I'm very sorry," Leigh said. His voice was deep, pleasant. "I must apologize. I thought-well, again I apologize. I'm rather excited, I'm afraid. You see, I've come from San Francisco to see this Witch Room of yours. Would you really mind letting me see it? I should be glad to pay any sum —"

Carson made a deprecatory gesture.

"No," he said, feeling a perverse liking for this man growing within him-his well-modulated, pleasant voice, his powerful face, his magnetic personality. "No, I merely want a little peace-you have no idea how I've been bothered," he went on, vaguely surprised to find himself speaking apologetically. "It's a frightful nuisance. I almost wish I'd never found the room."

Leigh leaned forward anxiously. "May I see it? It means a great deal to me —I'm vitally interested in these things. I promise not to take up more than ten minutes of your time."

Carson-hesitated, then assented. As he led his guest into the cellar he found himself telling the circumstances of his discovery of the Witch Room. Leigh listened intently, occasionally interrupting with questions.

"The rat-did you see what became of it?" he asked.

Carson looked bemused. "Why, no. I suppose it hid in its burrow. Why?"

"One never knows," Leigh said cryptically as they came into the Witch Room.

Carson switched on the light. He had had an electrical extension installed, and there were a few chairs and a table, but otherwise, the chamber was unchanged. Carson watched the occultist's face, and with surprise saw it become grim, almost angry.

Leigh strode to the center of the room, staring at the chair that stood on the black circle of stone. "You work here?" he asked slowly.

"Yes. It's quiet—I found I couldn't work upstairs. Too noisy. But this is ideal-somehow I find it very easy to write here. My mind feels"—he hesitated—"free; that is, disassociated with other things. It's quite an unusual feeling."

Leigh nodded as though Carson's words had confirmed some idea in his own mind. He turned toward the alcove and the metal disk in the floor. Carson followed him. The occultist moved close to the wall, tracing out the faded symbols with a long forefinger. He muttered something under his breath-words that sounded like gibberish to Carson.

"Nyogtha . . . k'yarnak..."

He swung about, his face grim and pale. "I've seen enough," he said softly. "Shall we go?" Surprised, Carson nodded and led the way back into the cellar.

Upstairs Leigh hesitated, as though finding it difficult to broach his subject. At length he asked, "Mr. Carson-would you mind telling me if you have had any peculiar dreams lately."

Carson stared at him, mirth dancing in his eyes. "Dreams?" he repeated. "Oh —I see. Well, Mr. Leigh, I may as well tell you that you can't frighten me. Your compatriots-the other occultists I've tertained — have already tried it."

Leigh raised his thick eyebrows. "Yes? Did they ask you whether you'd dreamed?"

"Several did-yes."

"And you told them?"

"No." Then as Leigh leaned back in his chair, a puzzled expression on his face, Carson went on slowly, "Although, really, I'm not quite sure."

"You mean?"

"I think —I have a vague impression-that I have dreamed lately. But I can't be sure. I can't remember anything of the dream, you see. And-oh, very probably your brother occultists put the idea into my mind!"

"Perhaps," Leigh said non-committally, getting up. He hesitated. "Mr. Carson, I'm going to ask you a rather presumptuous question. Is it necessary for you to live in this house?"

Carson sighed resignedly. "When I was first asked that question I explained that I wanted a quiet place to work on a novel, and that any quiet place would do. But it isn't easy to find 'em. Now that I have this Witch Room, and I'm turning out my work so easily, I see no reason why I should move and perhaps upset my program. I'll vacate this house when I finish my novel, and then you occultists can come in and turn it into a museum or do whatever you want with it. I don't care. But until the novel is finished I intend to stay here."

Leigh rubbed his chin. "Indeed. I can understand your point of view. But-is there no other place in the house where you can work?" He watched Carson's face for a moment, and then went on swiftly.

"I don't expect you to believe me. You are a materialist. Most people are. But there are a few of us who know that above and beyond what men call science there is a greater science that is built on laws and principles which to the average man would be almost incomprehensible. If you have read Machen you will remember that he speaks of the gulf between the world of consciousness and the world of matter. It is possible to bridge that gulf. The Witch Room is such a bridge! Do you know what a whispering-gallery is?"

"Eh?" Carson said, staring. "But there's no —"

"An analogy-merely an analogy. A man may whisper a word in gallery-or a cave-and if you are standing in a certain spot a hundred feet away you will hear that whisper, although someone ten feet away will not. It's a simple trick of acoustics-bringing the sound to a focal point. And this principle can be applied to other things besides sound. To any wave impulse-even to thought!"

Carson tried to interrupt, but Leigh kept on.

"That black stone in the center of your Witch Room is one of those focal points. The design on the floor-when you sit on the black circle there you are abnormally sensitive to certain vibrations — certain thought commands-dangerously sensitive! Why do you suppose your mind is so clear when you are working there? A deception, a false feeling of lucidity-for you are merely an instrument, a microphone, tuned to pick up certain malign vibrations the nature of which you could not comprehend!"

Carson's face Was a study in amazement and incredulity. "But-you don't mean you actually believe —"

Leigh drew back, the intensity fading from his eyes, leaving them grim and cold. "Very well. But I have studied the history of your Abigail Prinn. She, too, understood the super-science of which I speak. She used it for evil purposes-the black art, as it is called. I have read that she cursed Salem in the old days-and a witch's curse can be a frightful thing. Will you —" He got up, gnawing at his lip.

"Will you, at least, allow me to call on you tomorrow?"

Almost involuntarily Carson nodded. "But I'm afraid you'll be wasting your time. I don't believe —I mean, I have no —" He stumbled, at a loss for words.

"I merely wish to assure myself that you-oh, another thing. If you dream tonight, will you try to remember the dream? If you attempt to recapture it immediately after waking, it is often possible to recall it."

"All right. If I dream —"

That night Carson dreamed. He awoke just before dawn with his heart racing furiously and a curious feeling of uneasiness. Within the walls and from below he could hear the furtive scurryings of the rats. He got out of bed hastily, shivering in the cold grayness of early morning. A wan moon still shone faintly in a paling sky.

Then he remembered Leigh's words. He had dreamed-there was no question of that. But the content of his dream-that was another matter. He absolutely could not recall it to his mind, much as he tried, although there was a very vague impression of running frantically in darkness.

He dressed quickly, and because the stillness of early morning in the old house got on his nerves, went out to buy a newspaper. It was too early for shops to be open, however, and in search of a news-boy he set off westward, turning at the first corner. And as he walked a curious and inexplicable feeling began to take possession of him: a feeling of-familiarity! He had walked here before, and there was a dim and disturbing familiarity about the shapes of the houses, the outline of the roofs. But-and this was the fantastic part of it-to his knowledge he had never been on this street before. He had spent little time walking about this region of Salem, for he was indolent by nature; yet there was this extraordinary feeling of remembrance, and it grew more vivid as he went on.

He reached a corner, turned unthinkingly to the left. The odd sensation increased. He walked on slowly, pondering.

No doubt he had traveled by this way before-and very probably he had done so in a brown study, so that he had not been conscious of his route. Undoubtedly that was the explanation. Yet as Carson turned into Charter Street he felt a nameless unease waking within him. Salem was rousing; with daylight impassive Polish workers began to hurry past him toward the mills. An occasional automobile went by.

Before him a crowd was gathered on the sidewalk. He hastened his steps, conscious of a feeling of impending calamity. With an extraordinary sense of shock he saw that he was passing the Charter Street Burying Ground, the ancient, evilly famous "Burying Point." Hastily he pushed his way into the crowd.

Comments in a muffled undertone came to Carson's ears, and a bulky blue-clad back loomed up before him. He peered over the policeman's shoulder and caught his breath in a horrified gasp. man leaned against the iron railing that fenced the old graveyard. He wore a cheap, gaudy suit, and he gripped the rusty bars in a clutch that made the muscles stand out in ridges on the hairy backs of his hands. He was dead, and on his face, staring up at the sky at a crazy angle, was frozen an expression of abysmal and utterly shocking horror. His eyes, all whites, were bulging hideously; his mouth was a twisted, mirthless grin.

A man at Carson's side turned a white face toward him. "Looks as if he was scared to death," he said somewhat hoarsely. "I'd hate to have seen what he saw. Ugh-look at that face!"

Mechanically Carson backed away, feeling an icy breath of nameless things chill him. He rubbed his hand across his eyes, but still that contorted, dead face swam in his vision. He began to retrace his steps, shaken and trembling a little. Involuntarily his glance moved aside, rested on the tombs and monuments that dotted the old graveyard. No one had been buried there for over a century, and the lichen-stained tombstones, with their winged skulls, fat-cheeked cherubs, and funeral urns, seemed to breathe out an indefinable miasma of antiquity. What had frightened the man to death?

Carson drew a deep breath. True, the corpse had been a frightful spectacle, but he must not allow it to upset his nerves. He could not — his novel would suffer. Besides, he argued grimly to himself, the affair was obvious enough in its explanation. The dead man was apparently a Pole, one of the group of immigrants who dwell about Salem Harbor. Passing by the graveyard at night, a spot about which eldritch legends had clung for nearly three centuries, his drink-befuddled eyes must have given reality to the hazy phantoms of a superstitious mind. These Poles were notoriously unstable emotionally, prone to mob hysteria and wild imaginings. The great Immigrant Panic of 1853, in which three witch-houses had been burned to the ground, had grown from an old woman's confused and hysterical statement that she had seen a mysterious white-clad foreigner "take off his face." What else could be expected of such people, Carson thought?

Nevertheless he remained in a nervous state, and did not return home until nearly noon. When on his arrival he found Leigh, the occultist, waiting, he was glad to see the man, and invited him in with cordiality.

Leigh was very serious. "Did you hear about your friend Abigail Prinn?" he asked without preamble, and Carson stared, pausing in the act of siphoning charged water into a glass. After a long moment he pressed the lever, sent the liquid sizzling and foaming into the whiskey. He handed Leigh the drink and took one himself-neat — before answering the question.

"I don't know what you're talking about. Has-what's she been up to?" he asked, with an air of forced levity.

"I've been checking up the records," Leigh said, "and I find Abigail Prinn was buried on December 14th, 1690, in the Charter Street Burying Ground-with a stake through her heart. What's the matter?"

"Nothing," Carson said tonelessly. "Well?"

"Well-her grave's been opened and robbed, that's all. The stake was found uprooted nearby, and there were footprints all around the grave. Shoe-prints. Did you dream last night, Carson?" Leigh snapped out the question, his gray eyes hard.

"I don't know," Carson said confusedly, rubbing his forehead. "I can't remember. I was at the Charter Street graveyard this morning."

"Oh. Then you must have heard something about the man who —"

"I saw him," Carson interrupted, shuddering. "It upset me."

He downed the whiskey at a gulp.

Leigh watched him. "Well," he said presently, "are you still determined to stay in this house?" Carson put down the glass and stood up.

"Why not?" he snapped. "Is there any reason why I shouldn't? Eh?" "After what happened last night —"

"After what happened? A grave was robbed. A superstitious Pole saw the robbers and died of fright. Well?"

"You're trying to convince yourself," Leigh said calmly. "In your heart you know-you must know-the truth. You've become a tool in the hands of tremendous terrible forces, Carson. For three centuries Abbie Prinn has lain in her grave-undead-waiting for someone to fall into her trap-the Witch Room. Perhaps she foresaw the future when she built it, foresaw that someday someone would blunder into that hellish chamber and be caught by the trap of the mosaic pattern. It caught you, Carson-and enabled that undead horror to bridge the gulf between consciousness and matter, to get en rapport with you. Hypnotism is child's play to a being with Abigail Prinn's frightful powers. She could very easily force you to go to her grave and uproot the stake that held her captive, and then erase the memory of that act from your mind so that you could not remember it even as a dream!"

Carson was on his feet, his eyes burning with a strange light. "In God's name, man, do you know what you're saying?"

Leigh laughed harshly. "God's name! The devil's name, rather-the devil that menaces Salem at this moment; for Salem is in danger, terrible danger. The men and women and children of the town Abbie Prinn cursed when they bound her to the stake-and found they couldn't burn her! I've been going through certain secret archives this morning, and I've come to ask you, for the last time, to leave this house."

"Are you through?" Carson asked coldly. "Very well. I shall stay here. You're either insane or drunk, but you can't impress me with your poppycock."

"Would you leave if I offered you a thousand dollars?" Leigh asked. "Or more, then-ten thousand? I have a considerable sum at my command."

"No, damn it!" Carson snapped in a sudden blaze of anger. "All I want,is to be left alone to finish my novel. I can't work anywhere else —I don't want to, I won't —"

"I expected this," Leigh said, his voice suddenly quiet, and with a strange note of sympathy. "Man, you can't get away! You're caught in the trap, and it's too late for you to extricate yourself so long as Abbie Prinn's brain controls you through the Witch Room. And the worst part of it is that she can only manifest herself with your aid-she drains your life forces, Carson, feeds on you like a vampire." "You're mad," Carson said dully.

"I'm afraid. That iron disk in the Witch Room —I'm afraid of that, and what's under it. Abbie Prinn served strange gods, Carson-and I read something on the wall of that alcove that gave me a hint. Have you ever heard of Nyogtha?"

Carson shook his head impatiently. Leigh fumbled in a pocket, drew out a scrap of paper. "I copied this from a book in the Kester Library," he said, "a book called the Necronomicon, written by a man who delved so deeply into forbidden secrets that men called him mad. Read this."

Carson's brows drew together as he read the excerpt:

Men know him as the Dweller in Darkness, that brother of the Old Ones called Nyogtha, the Thing that should not be. He can be summoned to Earth's surface through certain secret caverns and fissures, and sorcerers have seen him in Syria and below the black tower of Leng; from the Thang Grotto of Tartary he has come ravening to bring terror and destruction among the pavilions of the great Khan. Only by the looped cross, by the Vach-Viraj incantation, and by the Tikkoun elixir may he be driven back to the nighted caverns of hidden foulness where he dwelleth.

Leigh met Carson's puzzled gaze calmly. "Do you understand now?" "Incantations and elixirs!" Carson said, handing back the paper.

"Fiddlesticks!"

"Far from it. That incantation and that elixir have been known to occultists and adepts for thousands of years. I've had occasion to use them myself in the past on certain-occasions. And if I'm right about this thing —" He turned to the door, his lips compressed in a bloodless line. "Such manifestations have been defeated before, but the difficulty lies in obtaining the elixir-it's very hard to get. But I hope . . . I'll be back. Can you stay out of the Witch Room until then?"

"I'll promise nothing," Carson said. He had a dull headache, which had been steadily growing until it obtruded upon his consciousness, and he felt vaguely nauseated. "Good-bye."

He saw Leigh to the door and waited on the steps, with an odd reluctance to return to the house. As he watched the tall occultist hurry down the street, a woman came out of the adjoining house. She caught sight of him, and her huge breasts heaved. She burst into a shrill, angry tirade.

Carson turned, staring at her with astonished eyes. His head throbbed painfully. The woman was approaching, shaking a fat fist threateningly.

"Why you scare my Sarah?" she cried, her swarthy face flushed. "Why you scare her wit' your fool tricks, eh?" Carson moistened his lips.

"I'm sorry," he said slowly. "Very sorry. I didn't frighten your Sarah. I haven't been home all day. What frightened her?"

"T'e brown t'ing-it ran in your house, Sarah say —"

The woman paused, and her jaw dropped. Her eyes widened. She made a peculiar sign with her right hand-pointing her index and little fingers at Carson, while her thumb was crossed over the other fingers. "T'e old witch!"

She retreated hastily, muttering in Polish in a frightened voice.

Carson turned, went back into the house. He poured some whiskey into a tumbler, considered, and then set it aside untasted. He began to pace the floor, occasionally rubbing his forehead with fingers that felt dry and hot. Vague, confused thoughts raced through his mind. His head was throbbing and feverish.

At length he went down to the Witch Room. He remained there, although he did not work; for his headache was not so oppressive in the dead quiet of the underground chamber. After a time he slept.

How long he slumbered he did not know. He dreamed of Salem, and of a dimly glimpsed, gelatinous black thing that hurtled with frightful speed through the streets, a thing like an incredibly huge, jet-black amoeba that pursued and engulfed men and women who shrieked and fled vainly. He dreamed of a skull-face peering into his own, a withered and shrunken countenance in which only the eyes seemed alive, and they shone with a hellish and evil light.

He awoke at last, sat up with a start. He was very cold.

It was utterly silent. In the light of the electric bulb the green and purple mosaic seemed to writhe and contract toward him, an illusion which disappeared as his sleep-fogged vision cleared. He glanced at his wrist-watch. It was two o'clock. He had slept through the afternoon and the better part of the night.

He felt oddly weak, and a lassitude held him motionless in his chair. The strength seemed to have been drained from him. The piercing cold seemed to strike through to his brain, but his headache was gone. His mind was very clear-expectant, as though waiting for something to happen. A movement nearby caught his eye.

A slab of stone in the wall was moving. He heard a gentle grating sound, and slowly a black cavity widened from a narrow rectangle to a square. There was something crouching there in the shadow. Stark, blind horror struck through Carson as the thing moved and crept forward into the light.

It looked like a mummy. For an intolerable, age-long second the thought pounded frightfully at Carson's brain: It looked like a mummy! It was a skeleton-thin, parchment-brown corpse, and it looked like a skeleton with the hide of some great lizard stretched over its bones. It stirred, it crept forward, and its long nails scratched audibly against the stone. It crawled out into the Witch Room, its passionless face pitilessly revealed in the white light, and its eyes were gleaming with charnel life. He could see the serrated ridge of its brown, shrunken back. . . .

Carson sat motionless. Abysmal horror had robbed him of the power to move. He seemed to be caught in the fetters of dream-paralysis, in which the brain, an aloof spectator, is unable or unwilling to transmit the nerve-impulses to the muscles. He told himself frantically that he was dreaming, that he would presently awaken.

The withered horror arose. It stood upright, skeleton-thin, and moved to the alcove where the iron disk lay embedded in the floor. Standing with its back to Carson it paused, and a dry and sere whisper rustled out in the dead stillness. At the sound Carson would have screamed, but he could not. Still the dreadful whisper went on, in a language Carson knew was not of Earth, and as though in response an almost imperceptible quiver shook the iron disk.

It quivered and began to rise, very slowly, and as if in triumph the shriveled horror lifted its pipestem arms. The disk was nearly a foot thick, but presently as it continued to rise above the level of the floor an insidious odor began to penetrate the room. It was vaguely reptilian, musky and nauseating. The disk lifted inexorably, and a little finger of blackness crept out from beneath its edge. Abruptly Carson remembered his dream of a gelatinous black creature that hurtled through the Salem streets. He tried vainly to break the fetters of paralysis that held him motionless. The chamber was darkening, and a black vertigo was creeping up to engulf him. The room seemed to rock. Still the iron disk lifted; still the withered horror stood with its skeleton arms raised in blasphemous benediction; still the blackness oozed out in slow amoeboid movement.

There came a sound breaking through the sere whisper of the mummy, the quick patter of racing footsteps. Out of the corner of his eye Carson saw a man come racing into the Witch Room. It was the occultist, Leigh, and his eyes were blazing in a face of deathly pallor. He flung himself past Carson to the alcove where the black horror was surging into view.

The withered thing turned with dreadful slowness. Leigh carried some implement in his left hand, Carson saw, a crux ansata of gold and ivory. His right hand was clenched at his side. His voice rolled out, sonorous and commanding. There were little beads of perspiration on his white face.

"Ya na kadishtu nil gh'ri . . . stell'bsna kn'aa Nyogtha . . . k'yarnak phlegethor...."

The fantastic, unearthly syllables thundered out, echoing from the walls of the vault. Leigh advanced slowly, the crux ansata held high.

And from beneath the iron disk black horror came surging!

The disk was lifted, flung aside, and a great wave of iridescent blackness, neither liquid nor solid, a frightful gelatinous mass, came pouring straight for Leigh. Without pausing in his advance he made a quick gesture with his right hand, and a little glass tube hurtled at the black thing, was engulfed.

The formless horror paused. It hesitated, with a dreadful air of indecision, and then swiftly drew back. A choking stench of burning corruption began to pervade the air, and Carson saw great pieces of the black thing flake off, shriveling as though destroyed with corroding acid. It fled back in a liquescent rush, hideous black flesh dropping as it retreated.

A pseudopod of blackness elongated itself from the central mass and like a great tentacle clutched the corpse-like being, dragged it back to the pit and over the brink. Another tentacle seized the iron disk, pulled it effortlessly across the floor, and as the horror sank from sight, the disk fell into place with a thunderous crash.

The room swung in wide circles about Carson, and a frightful nausea clutched him. He made a tremendous effort to get to his feet, and then the light faded swiftly and was gone. Darkness took him.

Carson's novel was never finished. He burned it, but continued to write, although none of his later work was ever published. His publishers shook their heads and wondered why such a brilliant writer of popular fiction had suddenly become infatuated with the weird and ghastly.

"It's powerful stuff," one man told Carson, as he handed back his novel, Black God of Madness. "It's remarkable in its way, but it's morbid and horrible. Nobody would read it. Carson, why don't you write the type of novel you used to do, the kind that made you famous?"

It was then that Carson broke his vow never to speak of the Witch Room, and he poured out the entire story, hoping for understanding and belief. But as he finished, his heart sank as he saw the other's face, sympathetic but skeptical.

"You dreamed it, didn't you?" the man asked, and Carson laughed bitterly.

"Yes —I dreamed it."

"It must have made a terribly vivid impression on your mind. Some dreams do. But you'll forget about it in time," he predicted, and Carson nodded.

And because he knew that he would only be arousing doubts of his sanity, he did not mention the thing that was burned indelibly on his brain, the horror he had seen in the Witch Room after wakening from his faint. Before he and Leigh had hurried, white-faced and trembling, from the chamber, Carson had cast a quick glance behind him. The shriveled and corroded patches that he had seen slough off from that being of insane blasphemy had unaccountably disappeared, although they had left black stains upon the stones. Abbie Prinn, perhaps, had returned to the hell she had served, and her inhuman god had withdrawn to hidden abysses beyond man's comprehension, routed by powerful forces of elder magic which the occultist had commanded. But the witch had left a memento behind her, a hideous thing which Carson, in that last backward glance, had seen protruding from the edge of the iron disk, as though raised in ironic salute —a withered, claw-like hand!

The Shadow on the Screen

A weird story of Hollywood, and the grisly horror that cast its dreadful shadow across the stiver screen as an incredible motion-picture was run off

Torture Master was being given a sneak preview at a Beverly Hills theatre. Somehow, when my credit line, "Directed by Peter Haviland," was flashed on the screen, a little chill of apprehension shook me, despite the applause that came from a receptive audience. When you've been in the picture game for a long time you get these hunches; I've often spotted a dud flicker before a hundred feet have been reeled off. Yet *Torture Master* was no worse than a dozen similar films I'd handled in the past few years.

But it was formula, box-office formula. 1 could see that. The star was all right; the make-up department had done a good job; the dialogue was unusually smooth. Yet the film was obviously box-office, and not the sort of film I'd have liked to direct.

After watching a reel unwind amid an encouraging scattering of applause, I got up and went to the lobby. Some of the gang from Summit Pictures were lounging there, smoking and commenting on the picture, Ann Howard, who played the heroine in *Torture Master*, noticed my scowl and pulled me into a corner. She was that rare type, a girl who will screen well without a lot of the yellow grease-paint that makes you look like an animated corpse. She was small, and her ha,ir and eyes and skin were brown —I'd like to have seen her play *Peter Pan*. That type, you know.

I had occasionally proposed to her, but she never took me seriously. As a matter of fact, I myself didn't know how serious I was about it. Now she led me into the bar and ordered sidecars.

"Don't look so miserable, Pete," she said over the rim of her glass. "The picture's going over. It'll gross enough to suit the boss, and it won't hurt my reputation."

Well, that was right. Ann had a fat part, and she'd made the most of it. And the picture would be good box-office; Universal's *Night Key*, with Karloff, had been released a few months ago, and the audiences were ripe for another horror picture.

"I know," I told her. signaling the bartender to refill my glass. "But I get tired of these damn hokumy pics. Lord, how I'd like to do another *Cabinet of Doctor Caligari!*"

"Or another *Ape of God*," Ann suggested.

I shrugged. "Even that, maybe. There's so much chance for development of the weird on the screen, Ann-and no producer will stand for a genuinely good picture of that type. They call it arty, and say it'll flop. If I branched out on my own-well, Hecht and MacArthur tried it, and they're back on the Hollywood payroll now."

Someone Ann knew came up and engaged her in conversation. I saw a man beckoning, and with a hasty apology left Ann to join him. It was Andy Worth, Hollywood's dirtiest columnist. I knew him for a double-crosser and a skunk, but I also knew that he could get more inside information than a brace of Winchells. He was a short, fat chap with a meticulously cultivated mustache and sleeky pomaded black hair. Worth fancied himself as a ladies' man, and spent a great deal of his time trying to blackmail actresses into having affairs with him.

That didn't make him a villain, of course. I like anybody who can carry on an intelligent conversation for ten minutes, and Worth could do that. He fingered his mustache and said, "I heard you talking about *Ape of God*, A coincidence, Pete."

"Yeah?" I was cautious. I had to be, with this walking scandal-sheet. "How's that?"

He took a deep breath. "Well, you understand that I haven't got the real lowdown, and it's all hearsay-but I've found a picture that'll make the weirdest flicker ever canned look side"

I suspected a gag. "Okay, what is it? *Torture Master?*"

"He was lifted through a welter of coiling, ropy tentacles."

"Eh? No-though Blake's yarn deserved better adaptation than your boys gave it. No, Pete, the one I'm talking about isn't for general release-isn't completed, in fact. I saw a few rushes of it. A one-man affair; title's *The Nameless*. Arnold Keene's doing it."

Worth sat back and watched how I took that. And I must have shown my amazement. For it was Arnold Keene who had directed the notorious *Ape of God*, which had wrecked his promising career in films. The public doesn't know that picture. It never was released. Summit junked it. And they had good cause, although it was one of the most amazingly effective weird films I've ever seen. Keene had shot most of it down in Mexico, and he'd been able to assume virtual dictatorship of the location troupe. Several Mexicans had died at the time, and there had been some ugly rumors, but it had all been hushed up. I'd talked with several people who had been down near Taxco with Keene, and they spoke of the man with peculiar horror. He had been willing to sacrifice almost anything to make *Ape of God* a masterpiece of its type.

It was an unusual picture-there was no question about that. There's only one master print of the film, and it's kept in a locked vault at Summit. Very few have seen it. For what Machen had done in weird literature, Keene had done on the screen-and it was literally amazing.

I said to Worth, "Arnold Keene, eh? I've always had a sneaking sympathy for the man. But I thought he'd died long ago."

"Oh, no. He bought a place near Tujunga and went into hiding. He didn't have much dough after the blow-up, you know, and it took him about five years to get together enough *dinero* to start his *Nameless*. He always said *Ape of God* was a failure, and that he intended to do a film that would be a masterpiece of weirdness. Well, he's done it. He's canned a film that's —unearthly. I tell you it made my flesh creep."

"Who's the star?" I asked.

"Unknowns. Russian trick, you know. The real star is a —a shadow."

I stared at him.

"That's right, Pete. The shadow of something that's never shown on the screen. Doesn't sound like much, eh? But you ought to see it!"

"I'd like to," I told him. "In fact, I'll do just that. Maybe he'll release it through Summit."

Worth chuckled. "No chance. No studio would release that flicker. I'm not even going to play it up in my dirt sheet. This is the real McCoy, Pete."

"What's Keene's address?" I asked.

Worth gave it to me. "But don't go out till Wednesday night," he said. "The rough prints'll be ready then, or most of them. And keep it under you hat, of course."

A group of autograph hunters came up just then, and Worth and I were separated. It didn't matter. I'd got all the information I needed. My mind was seething with fantastic surmises. Keene was one of the great geniuses of the screen, and his talent lay in the direction of the macabre. Unlike book publishers, the studios catered to no small, discriminating audiences. A film must suit everybody.

Finally I broke away and took Ann to a dance at Bel-Air. But I hadn't forgotten Keene, and the next night I was too impatient to wait. I telephoned Worth, but he was out. Oddly enough, I was unable to get in touch with him during the next few days; even his paper couldn't help me. A furious editor told me the Associated Press had been sending him hourly telegrams asking for Worth's copy; but the man had vanished completely. I had a hunch.

It was Tuesday night when I drove out of the studio and took a short cut through Griffith Park, past the Planetarium, to Glendale. From there I went on to Tujunga, to the address Worth had given me. Once or twice I had an uneasy suspicion that a black coupe was trailing me. but I couldn't be sure.

Arnold Keene's house was in a little canyon hidden back in the Tujunga mountains. I had to follow a winding dirt road for several miles, and ford a stream or two, before I reached it. The place was built against the side of the canyon, and a man stood on the porch and watched me as I braked my car to a stop.

It was Arnold Keene. I recognized him immediately. He was a slender man under middle height, with a closely cropped bristle of gray hair; his face was coldly austere. There had been a rumor that Keene had at one time been an officer in Prussia before he came to Hollywood and Americanized his name, and, scrutinizing him, I could well believe it. His eyes were like pale blue marbles, curiously shallow.

He said, "Peter Haviland? I did not expect you until tomorrow night."

I shook hands. "Sorry if I intrude," I apologized. "The fact is, I got impatient after what Worth told me about your film. He isn't here, by any chance?"

The shallow eyes were unreadable. "No. But come in. Luckily, the developing took less time than I had anticipated. I need only a few more shots to complete my task."

He ushered me into the house, which was thoroughly modern and comfortably furnished. Under the influence of good cognac my suspicions began to dissolve. I told Keene I had always admired his *Ape of God*.

He made a wry grimace. "Amateurish, Haviland. I depended too much on hokum in that film. Merely devil-worship, a reincarnated Gilles de Rais, and sadism. That isn't true weirdness."

I was interested. "That's correct. But the film had genuine power — —"

"Man has nothing of the weird in him intrinsically. It is only the hints of the utterly abnormal and unhuman that give one the true feeling of weirdness. That, and human reactions to such supernatural phenomena. Look at any great weird work-The Horla, which tells of a man's reaction to a creature utterly alien, Blackwood's Willows, Machen's Black Seal, Lovecraft's Color Out of Space-all these deal with the absolutely alien influencing normal lives, Sadism and death may contribute, but alone they cannot produce the true, intangible atmosphere of weirdness."

I had read all these tales. "But you can't film the indescribable. How could you show the invisible beings of The Willows?"

Keene hesitated. "I think I'll let my film answer that. I have a projection room downstairs —"

The bell rang sharply. I could not help noticing the quick glance Keene darted at me. With an apologetic gesture he went out and presently returned with Ann Howard at his side. She was smiling rather shakily.

"Did you forget our date, Pete?" she asked me.

I blinked, and suddenly remembered. Two weeks ago I had promised to take Ann to an affair in Laguna Beach this evening, but in my preoccupation with Keene's picture the date had slipped my mind. I stammered apologies.

"Oh, that's all right," she broke in. "I'd much rather stay here-that is, if Mr. Keene doesn't mind. His picture — —"

"You know about it?"

"I told her," Keene said. "When she explained why she had come, I took the liberty of inviting her to stay to watch the film. I did not want her to drag you away, you see," he finished, smiling. "Some cognac for Miss-eh?"

I introduced them.

"For Miss Howard, and then *The Nameless*."

At his words a tiny warning note seemed to throb in my brain. I had been fingering a heavy metal paperweight, and now, as Keene's attention was momentarily diverted to the sideboard, I slipped it, on a sudden impulse, into my pocket. It would be no defense, though, against a gun.

What was wrong with me, I wondered? An atmosphere of distrust and suspicion seemed to have sprung out of nothing. As Keene ushered us down into his projection room, the skin of my back seemed to crawl with the expectation of attack. It was inexplicable, but definitely unpleasant.

Keene was busy for a time in the projection booth, and then he joined us.

"Modern machinery is a blessing," he said with heavy jocularity. "I can be as lazy as I wish. I needed no help with the shooting, once the automatic cameras were installed. The projector, too, is automatic."

I felt Ann move closer to me in the gloom. I put my arm around her and said, "It helps, yes. What about releasing the picture, Mr. Keene?"

There was a harsh note in his voice. "It will not be released. The world is uneducated, not ready for it. In a hundred years, perhaps, it will achieve the fame it deserves. I am doing it for posterity, and for the sake of creating a weird masterpiece on the screen."

With a muffled click the projector began to operate, and a title flashed on the screen: *The Nameless*.

Keene's voice came out of the darkness. "It's a silent film, except for one sequence at the start. Sound adds nothing to weirdness, and it helps to destroy the illusion of reality. Later, suitable music will be dubbed in."

I did not answer. For a book had flashed on the gray oblong before us-that amazing tour de force, *The Circus of Doctor Lao*. A hand opened it, and a long finger followed the lines as a toneless voice read:

"These are the sports, the offthrows of the universe instead of the species; these are the weird children of the lust of the spheres. Mysticism explains them where science cannot. Listen: when that great mysterious fecundity that peopled the worlds at the command of the gods had done with its birth-giving, when the celestial midwives all had left, when life had begun in the universe, the primal womb-thing found itself still unexhausted, its loins stiil potent. So that awful fertility tossed on its couch in a final fierce outbreak of life-giving and gave birth to these nightmare beings, these abortions of the world."

The voice ceased. The book faded, and there swam into view a mass of tumbled ruins. The ages had pitted the man-carved rocks with cracks and scars; the bas-relief figures were scarcely recognizable. I was reminded of certain ruins I had seen in Yucatan.

The camera swung down. The ruins seemed to grow larger. A yawning hole gaped in the earth.

Beside me Keene said, "The site of a ruined temple. Watch, now."

The effect was that of moving forward into the depths of a subterranean pit For a moment the screen was in darkness; then a stray beam of sunlight rested on an idol that stood in what was apparently an underground cavern. A narrow crack of light showed in the roof. The idol was starkly hideous.

I got only a flashing glimpse, but the impression on my mind was that of a bulky, ovoid shape like a pineapple or a pine-cone. The thing had certain doubtful features which lent it a definitely unpleasant appearance; but it was gone in a flash, dissolving into a brightly lighted drawing-room, thronged with gay couples.

The story proper began at that point. None of the actors or actresses was known to me; Keene must have hired them and worked secretly in his house. Most of the interiors and a few of the exteriors seemed to have been taken in this very canyon. The director had used the "parallel" trick which saves so much money for studios yearly. I'd often done it myself. It simply means that the story is tied in with real life as closely as possible; that is, when I had a troupe working up at Lake Arrowhead last winter, and an unexpected snowfall changed the scene, I had the continuity rewritten so that the necessary scenes could take place in snow. Similarly, Keene had paralleled his own experiences-sometimes almost too closely.

The Nameless told of a man, ostracized by his fellows because of his fanatical passion for the morbid and bizarre, who determined to create a work of art —a living masterpiece of sheer weirdness. He had experimented before by directing films that were sufficiently unusual to stir up considerable comment. But this did not satisfy him. It was acting-and he wanted something more than that. No one can convincingly fake reaction to horror, not even the most talented actor, he contended. The genuine emotion must be felt in order to be transferred to the screen.

It was here that *The Nameless* ceased to parallel Keene's own experiences, and branched out into sheer fantasy. The protagonist in the film was Keene himself, but this was not unusual, as directors often act in their own productions. And, by deft montage shots, the audience learned that Keene in his search for authenticity had gone down into Mexico, and had, with the aid of an ancient scroll, found the site of a ruined Aztec temple. And here, as I say, reality was left behind as the film entered a morbid and extraordinary phase.

There was a god hidden beneath this ruined temple —a long-forgotten god, which had been worshipped even before the Aztecs had sprung from the womb of the centuries. At least, the natives had considered it a god, and had erected a temple in its honor, but Keene hinted that the thing was actually a survival, one of the "offthrows of the universe," unique and baroque, which had come down through the eons in an existence totally alien to mankind. The creature was never actually seen on the screen, save for a few brief glimpses in the shadowed, underground temple. It was roughly barrel-shaped, and perhaps ten feet high, studded with odd spiky projections. The chief feature was a gem set in the thing's rounded apex —a smoothly polished jewel as large as a child's head. It was in this gem that the being's life was supposed to have its focus.

It was not dead, but neither was it alive, in the accepted sense of that term. When the Aztecs had filled the temple with the hot stench of blood the thing had lived, and the jewel had flamed with unearthly radiance. But with the passage of time the sacrifices had ceased, and the being had sunk into a state of coma akin to hibernation. In the picture Keene brought it to life.

He transported it secretly to his home, and there, in an underground room hollowed beneath the house, he placed the monster-god. The room was built with an eye for the purpose for whidi Keene intended it: automatic cameras and clever lighting features were installed, so that pictures could be shot from several different angles at once, and pieced together later as Keene cut the film. And now there entered something of the touch of genius which had made Keene famous.

He was clever, I had always realized that. Yet in the scenes that were next unfolded I admired not so much the technical tricks-which were familiar enough to me-as the marvelously clever way in which Keene had managed to inject realism into the acting. His characters did not act-they *lived*

Or, rather, they died. For in the picture they were thrust into the underground room to die horribly as sacrifices to the monster-god from the Aztec temple. Sacrifice was supposed to bring the thing to life, to cause the jewel in which its existence was bound to flare with fantastic splendor. The first sacrifice was, I think, the most effective.

The underground room in which the god was hidden was large, but quite vacant, save for a curtained alcove which held the idol. A barred doorway led to the upper room, and here Keene appeared on the screen, revolver in hand, herding before him a man-overall-clad, with a stubble of black beard on his stolid face. Keene swung open the door, motioned his captive into the great room. He closed the barred door, and through the grating could be seen busy at a switchboard.

Light flared. The man stood near the bars, and then, at Keene's gesture with his weapon, moved forward slowly to the far wall, He stood there, staring around vaguely, dull apprehension in his face. Light threw his shadow in bold relief on the wall.

Then another shadow leaped into existence beside him.

It was barrel-shaped, gigantic, studded with blunt spikes, and capped by a round dark blob-the life-jewel. The shadow of the monster god! The man saw it. He turned.

Stark horror sprang into his face, and at sight of that utterly ghastly and realistic expression a chill struck through me. This was almost too convincing. The man could not be merely acting. But, if he was, his acting was superb, and so was Keene's direction. The shadow on the wall stirred, and a thrill of movement shook it. It rocked and seemed to rise, supported by a dozen tentacular appendages that uncoiled from beneath its base. The spikes-changed. They lengthened. They coiled and writhed, hideously worm-like.

It wasn't the metamorphosis of the shadow that held me motionless in my chair. Rather, it was the appalling expression of sheer horror on the man's face. He stood gaping as the shadow toppled and swayed on the wall, growing larger and larger. Then he fled, his mouth an open square of terror. The shadow paused, with an odd air of indecision, and slipped slowly along the wall out of range of the camera.

But there were other cameras, and Keene had used his cutting-shears deftly. The movements of the man were mirrored on the screen; the glaring lights swung and flared; and ever the grim shadow crawled hideously across the wall. The thing that cast it was never shown-just the shadow, and it was a dramatically effective trick. Too many directors, I knew, could not have resisted the temptation to show the monster, thus destroying the illusion-for papier-mache and rubber, no matter how cleverly constructed, cannot convincingly ape reality.

At last the shadows merged-the gigantic swaying thing with its coiling tentacles, and the black shadow of the man that was caught and lifted, struggling and kicking frantically. The shadows merged-and the man did not reappear. Only the dark blob capping the great shadow faded and flickered, as though strange light were streaming from it; the light that was fed by sacrifice, the jewel that was-life.

Beside me there came a rustle. I felt Ann stir and move closer in the gloom. Keene's voice came from some distance away.

"There were several more sacrifice scenes, Haviland, but I haven't patched them in yet, except for the one you'll see in a moment now. As I said, the film isn't finished."

I did not answer. My eyes were on the screen as the fantastic tale unfolded. The pictured Keene was bringing another victim to his cavern, a short, fat man with sleekly pomaded black hair. I did not see his face until he had been imprisoned in the cave, and then, abruptly, there came a close-up shot, probably done with a telescopic lens. His plump face, with its tiny mustache, leaped into gigantic visibility, and I recognized Andy Worth.

It was the missing columnist, but for the first time I saw his veneer of sophistication lacking. Naked fear crawled in his eyes, and I leaned forward in my seat as the ghastly barrel-shaped shadow sprang out on the wall. Worth saw it, and the expression on his face was shocking. I pushed back my chair and got up as the lights came on. The screen went blank.

Arnold Keene was staanding by the door, erect and military as ever. He had a gun in his hand, and its muzzle was aimed at my stomach.

"You had better sit down, Haviland," he said quietly. "You too, Miss Howard. I've something to tell you-and I don't wish to be melodramatic about it. This gun" —he glanced at it wryly —"is necessary. There are a few things you must know, Haviland, for a reason you'll understand later."

I said, "There'll be some visitors here for you soon, Keene. You don't think I'd neglect normal precautions!"

He shrugged. "You're lying, of course. Also you're unarmed, or you'd have had your gun out by now. I didn't expect you until tomorrow night, but I'm prepared. In a word, what I have to tell you is this: the film you just saw is a record of actual events."

Ann's teeth sank into her lip, but I didn't say anything. I waited, and Keene resumed.

"Whether you believe me or not doesn't matter, for you'll have to believe in a few minutes. I told you something of my motive, my desire to create a genuine masterpiece of weirdness. That's what I've done, or will have done before tomorrow. Quite a number of vagrants and laborers have disappeared, and the columnist, Worth, as well; but I took care to leave no clues. You'll be the last to vanish-you and this girl."

"You'll never be able to show the film," I told him.

"What of it? You're a hack, Haviland, and you can't understand what it means to create a masterpiece. Is a work of art any less beautiful because it's hidden? I'll see the picture-and after I'm dead the world will see it, and realize my genius even though they may fear and hate its expression. The reactions of my unwilling actors-that's the trick. As a director, you should know that there's no substitute for realism. The reactions were not faked-that was obvious enough. The first sacrifice was that of a clod-an unintelligent moron, whose fears were largely superstitious. The next sacrifice was of a higher type —a vagrant who came begging to my door some months ago. You will complete the group, for you'll know just what you're facing, and your attempt to rationalize your fear will lend an interesting touch. Both of you will stand up, with your hands in the air, and precede me into this passage."

All this came out tonelessly and swiftly, quite as though it were a rehearsed speech. His hand slid over the wall beside him, and a black oblong widened in the oak paneling. I stood up.

"Do as he says, Ann," I said. "Maybe I can — —"

"No, you can't," Keene interrupted, gesturing impatiently with his weapon. "You won't have the chance. Hurry up."

We went through the opening in the wall and Keene followed, touching a stud that flooded the passage with light. It was a narrow tunnel that slanted down through solid rock for perhaps ten feet to a steep stairway. He herded us down this, after sliding the panel shut.

"It's well hidden," he said, indicating metal sheathing-indeed, the entire corridor was lined with metal plates. "This lever opens it from within, but no one but me can find the spring which opens it from without. The police could wreck the house without discovering this passage."

That seemed worth remembering, but of little practical value at the moment. Ann and I went down the stairway until it ended in another short passage. Our way was blocked by a door of steel bars, which Keene unlocked with a key he took from his pocket. The passage where we stood was dimly lighted; there were several chairs here; and the space beyond the barred door was not lighted at all.

Keene opened the door and gestured me through it. He locked it behind me and turned to Ann. Her face, I saw, was paper-white in the pale glow.

What happened after that brought an angry curse to my lips. Without warning Keene swung the automatic in a short. vicious arc, smashing it against Ann's head.

She saw it coming too late, and her upflung hand failed to ward off the blow. She dropped without a sound, a little trickle of blood oozing from her temple. Keene stepped over her body to a switchboard set in the rock wall.

Light lanced with intolerable brilliance into my eyes. I shut them tightly, opening them after a moment to stare around apprehensively. I recognized my surroundings. I was in the cave of sacrifice, the underground den I had seen on the screen. Cameras high up on the walls began to operate as I discovered them. From various points blinding arc-lights streamed down upon me.

A gray curtain shielded a space on the far wall, but this was drawn upward to reveal a deep alcove. There was an object within that niche—a barrel-shaped thing ten feet high, studded with spikes, and crowned with a jewel that pulsed and glittered with cold flame. It was gray and varnished-looking, and it was the original of Keene's Aztec god.

Somehow I felt oddly reassured as I examined the thing. It was a model, of course, inanimate and dead; for certainly no life of any kind could exist in such an abnormality. Keene might have installed machinery of some sort within it, however.

"You see, Haviland," Keene said from beyond the bars, "the thing actually exists. I got on the trail of it in an old parchment I found in the Huntington Library. It had been considered merely an interesting bit of folk-lore, but I saw something else in it. When I was making *Ape of God* in Mexico I discovered the ruined temple, and what lay forgotten behind the altar."

He touched a switch, and light streamed out from the alcove behind the thing. Swiftly I turned. On the wall behind me was my own shadow, grotesquely elongated, and beside it was the squat, amorphous patch of blackness I had seen on the screen upstairs.

My back was toward Keene, and my ringers crept into my pocket, touching the metal paper-weight I had dropped there earlier that evening. Briefly I considered the possibility of hurling the thing at Keene, and then decided against it. The bars were too close together, and the man would shoot me at any sign of dangerous hostility.

My eyes were drawn to the shadow on the wall. It was moving.

It rocked slightly, and lifted. The spikes lengthened. The thing was no longer inanimate and dead, and as I swung about, stark amazement gripping me, I saw the incredible metamorphosis that had taken place in the thing that cast the shadow.

It was no longer barrel-shaped. A dozen smooth, glistening appendages, ending in flat pads, supported the snake-thin body. And all over that grayish upright pole tentacles sprouted and lengthened, writhing into ghastly life as the horror awakened. Keene had not lied, and the monstrous survival he had brought from the Aztec temple was lumbering from the alcove, its myriad tentacles alive with frightful hunger!

Keene saved me. He saw me standing motionless with abysmal fear in the path of that gigantic, nightmare being, and realizing that he was being cheated of his picture, the man shouted at me to run. His hoarse voice broke the spell that held me unmoving, and I whirled and fled across the cave to the barred door. Skin ripped from my hands as I tore at the bars.

"Run!" Keene yelled at me, his shallow eyes blazing. "It can't move fast! Look out — —"

A writhing, snake-like thing lashed out, and a sickening musky stench filled my nostrils. I leaped away, racing across the cave again. The arc-lights died and others flared into being as Keene manipulated the switchboard. He was adjusting the lights, so that our shadows would not be lost-so that in the climax of *The Nameless* the shadow of that ghastly horror would be thrown on the cave wail beside me.

It was an infernal game of tag we played there, in those shifting Lights that glared down while the camera lenses watched dispassionately. I fled and dodged with my pulses thundering and blood pounding in my temples, and ever the grim shadow moved slowly across the walls, while my legs began to ache with the strain. For hours, perhaps, or eons, I fled.

There would come brief periods of respite when I would cling to the bars, cursing Keene, but he would not answer. His hands flickered over the switchboard as he adjusted the arc-lights, and his eyes never paused in their roving examination of the cave. In the end it was this that saved me.

For Keene did not see Ann stir and open her eyes. He did not see the girl, after a swift glance around, get quietly to her feet. Luckily she was behind Keene, and he did not turn.

I tried to keep my eyes away from Ann, but I do not think I succeeded. At the last moment I saw Keene's face change, and he started back; but the chair in Ann's hands crashed down and splintered on the man's head. He fell to his knees, clawing at the air, and then collapsed inertly.

I was on the far side of the cave, and my attention was momentarily diverted from the monster. I had been watching it from the corner of my eye, expecting to be able to dodge and leap away before it came too close; but it lumbered forward with a sudden burst of speed. Although I tried to spring clear I failed; a tentacle whipped about my legs and sent me sprawling. As I tried to roll away another smooth gray coil got my left arm.

Intolerable agony dug into my shoulder as I was lifted. I heard Ann scream, and a gun barked angrily. Bullets plopped into the smooth flesh of the monster, but it paid no attention. I was lifted through a welter of coiling, ropy tentacles, until just above me was the flaming jewel in which the creature's life was centered.

Remembrance of Keene's words spurred me to action; this might be the monster's vulnerable point. The paperweight was still in my pocket, and I clawed it out desperately. I hurled it with all my strength at the shining gem. And the jewel shattered!

There came a shrill vibration, like the tinkling of countless tiny crystalline bells. Piercingly sweet, it shrilled in my ears, and died away quickly. And suddenly nothing existed but light.

It was as though the shattering of the gem had released a sea of incandescent flame imprisoned within it. The glare of the arc-lights faded beside this flood of silvery radiance that bathed me. The cold glory of Arcturus, the blaze of tropical moonlight, were in the light.

Swiftly it faded and fled away. I felt myself dropping, and pain lanced into my wrenched shoulder as I struck the ground. I heard Ann's voice.

Dazedly I got up, expecting to see the monster towering above me. But it was gone. In its place, a few feet away, was the barrel-shaped thing I had first seen in the alcove. There was a gaping cavity in the rounded apex where the jewel had been. And, somehow, I sensed that the creature was no longer deadly, no longer a horror.

I saw Ann. She was still holding Keene's gun, and in her other hand was the key with which she had unlocked the door. She came running toward me, and I went swiftly to meet her.

I took the gun and made sure it was loaded. "Come on," I said, curtly. "We're getting out of here."

Ann's fingers were gripping my arm tightly as we went through the door, past the prone figure of Keene, and up the stairway. The lever behind the panel was not difficult to operate, and I followed Ann through the opening into the theater. Then I paused, listening.

Ann turned, watching me, a question in her eyes. "What is it, Pete?"

"Listen," I said. "Get the cans of film from the projection booth. We'll take them with us and burn them."

"But—you're not — —"

"I'll be with you in a minute," I told her, and swung the panel shut.

I went down the stairs swiftly and very quietly, my gun ready and my ears alert for the low muttering I had heard from below.

Keene was no longer unconscious. He was standing beside the switchboard with his back to me, and over his shoulder I could see the shadow of the monster-god sprawling on the wall, inert and lifeless. Keene was chanting something, in a language I did not know, and his hands were moving in strange gestures.

God knows what unearthly powers Keene had acquired in his search for horror! For as I stood there, watching the patch of blackness on the cave wall, I saw a little shudder rock that barrel-shaped shadow of horror, while a single spike abruptly lengthened into a tentacle that groped out furtively and drew back and vanished.

Then I killed Arnold Keene.

The Secret of Kralitz

A story of the shocking revelation that came to the twenty-first Baron Kralitz

I awoke from profound sleep to find two black-swathed forms standing silently beside me, their faces pale blurs in the gloom. As I blinked to clear my sleep-dimmed eyes, one of them beckoned impatiently, and suddenly I realized the purpose of this midnight summons. For years I had been expecting it, ever since my father, the Baron Kralitz, had revealed to me the secret and the curse that hung over our ancient house. And so, without a word, I rose and followed my guides as they led me along the gloomy corridors of the castle that had been my home since birth.

As I proceeded there rose up in my mind the stern face of my father, and in my ears rang his solemn words as he told me of the legendary curse of the House of Kralitz, the unknown secret that was imparted to the eldest son of each generation-at a certain time.

"When?" I had asked my father as he lay on his death-bed, fighting back the approach of dissolution.

"When you are able to understand," he had told me, watching my face intently from beneath his tufted white brows. "Some are told the secret sooner than others. Since the first Baron Kralitz the secret has been handed down — —"

He clutched at his breast and paused. It was fully five minutes before he had gathered his strength to speak again in his rolling, powerful voice. No gasping, death-bed confessions for the Baron Kralitz!

He said at last, "You have seen the ruins of the old monastery near the village, Franz. The first Baron burnt it and put the monks to the sword. The Abbot interfered too often with the Baron's whims. A girl sought shelter and the Abbot refused to give her up at the Baron's demand. His patience was at an end-you know the tales they still tell about him.

"He slew the Abbot, burned the monastery, and took the girl. Before he died the Abbot cursed his slayer, and cursed his sons for unborn generations. And it is the nature of this curse that is the secret of our house.

"I may not tell you what the curse is. Do not seek to discover it before it is revealed to you. Wait patiently, and in due time you will be taken by the warders of the secret down the stairway to the underground cavern. And then you will learn the secret of Kralitz."

As the last word passed my father's lips he died, his stern face still set in its harsh lines.

* * * * *

Deep in my memories, I had not noticed our path, but now the dark forms of my guides paused beside a gap in the stone flagging, where a stairway which I had never seen during my wanderings about the castle led into subterranean depths. Down this stairway I was conducted, and presently I came to realize that there was light of a sort —a dim, phosphorescent radiance that came from no recognizable source, and seemed to be less actual light than the accustoming of my eyes to the near-darkness.

I went down for a long time. The stairway turned and twisted in the rock, and the bobbing forms ahead were my only relief from the monotony of the interminable descent. And at last, deep underground, the long stairway ended, and I gazed over the shoulders of my guides at the great door that barred my path. It was roughly chiseled from the solid stone, and upon it were curious and strangely disquieting carvings, symbols which I did not recognize. It swung open, and I passed through and paused, staring about me through a gray sea of mist.

I stood upon a gentle slope that fell away into the fog-hidden distance, from which came a pandemonium of muffled bellowing and high-pitched, shrill squeakings vaguely akin to obscene laughter. Dark, half-glimpsed shapes swam into sight through the haze and disappeared again, and great vague shadows swept overhead on silent wings. Almost beside me was a long rectangular table of stone, and at this table two score of men were seated, watching me from eyes that gleamed dully out of deep sockets. My two guides silently took their places among them.

And suddenly the thick fog began to lift. It was swept raggedly away on the breath of a chill wind. The far dim reaches of the cavern were revealed as the mist swiftly dissipated, and I stood silent in the grip of a mighty fear, and, strangely, an equally potent, unaccountable thrill of delight. A part of my mind seemed to ask, "What horror is this?" And another part whispered, "You know this place!"

But I could never have seen it before. If I had realized what lay far beneath the castle I could never have slept at night for the fear that would have obsessed me. For, standing silent with conflicting tides of horror and ecstasy racing through me, I saw the weird inhabitants of the underground world.

Demons, monsters, unnamable things! Nightmare colossi strode bellowing through the murk, and amorphous gray things like giant slugs walked upright on stumpy legs. Creatures of shapeless soft pulp, beings with flame-shot eyes scattered over their misshapen bodies like fabled Argus, writhed and twisted there in the evil glow. Winged things that were not bats swooped and fluttered in the tenebrous air, whispering sibilantly-whispering in *human* voices.

Far away at the bottom of the slope I could see the chill gleam of water, a hidden, sunless sea. Shapes mercifully almost hidden by distance and the semi-darkness sported and cried, troubling the surface of the lake, the size of which I could only conjecture. And a flapping thing whose leathery wings stretched like a tent above my head swooped and hovered for a moment, staring with flaming eyes, and then darted off and was lost in the gloom.

And all the while, as I shuddered with fear and loathing, within me was this evil glee-this voice which whispered, "You know this place! You belong here! Is it not good to be home?"

I glanced behind me. The great door had swung silently shut, and escape was impossible. And then pride came to my aid. I was a Kralitz. And a Kralitz would not acknowledge fear in the face of the devil himself!

* * * * *

I stepped forward and confronted the warders, who were still seated regarding me intently from eyes in which a smoldering fire seemed to burn. Fighting down an insane dread that I might find before me an array of fleshless skeletons, I stepped to the head of the table, where there was a sort of crude throne, and peered closely at the silent figure on my right.

It was no bare skull at which I gazed, but a bearded, deadly-pale face. The curved, voluptuous lips were crimson, looking almost rouged, and the dull eyes stared through me bleakly. Inhuman agony had etched itself in deep lines on the white face, and gnawing anguish smoldered in the sunken eyes. I cannot hope to convey the utter strangeness, the atmosphere of unearthliness that surrounded him, almost as palpable as the fetid tomb-stench that welled from his dark garments. He waved a black-swathed arm to the vacant seat at the head of the table, and I sat down.

This nightmare sense of unreality! I seemed to be in a dream, with a hidden part of my mind slowly waking from sleep into evil life to take command of my faculties. The table was set with old-fashioned goblets and trenchers such as had not been used for hundreds of years. There was meat on the trenchers, and red liquor in the jeweled goblets. A heady, overpowering fragrance swam up into my nostrils, mixed with the grave-smell of my companions and the musty odor of a dank and sunless place.

Every white face was turned to me, faces that seemed oddly familiar, although I did not know why. Each face was alike in its blood-red, sensual lips and its expression of gnawing agony, and burning black eyes like the abysmal pits of Tartarus stared at me until I felt the short hairs stir on my neck. But —I was a Kralitz! I stood up and said boldly in archaic German that somehow came familiarly from my lips, "I am Franz, twenty-first Baron Kralitz. What do you want with me?"

A murmur of approval went around the long table. There was a stir. From the foot of the board a huge bearded man arose, a man with a frightful scar that made the left side of his face a horror of healed white tissue. Again the odd thrill of familiarity ran through me; I had seen that face before, and vaguely I remembered looking at it through dim twilight.

The man spoke in the old guttural German. "We greet you, Franz, Baron Kralitz. We greet you and pledge you, Franz-and we pledge the House of Kralitz!"

With that he caught up the goblet before him and held it high. All along the long table the black-swathed ones arose, and each held high his jeweled cup, and pledged me. They drank deeply, savoring the liquor, and I made the bow custom demanded. I said, in words that sprang almost unbidden from my mouth:

"I greet you, who are the warders of the secret of Kralitz, and I pledge you in return."

All about me, to the farthermost reaches of the dim cavern, a hush fell, and the bellows and howlings, and the insane tittering of the flying things, were no longer heard. My companions leaned expectantly toward me. Standing alone at the head of the board, I raised my goblet and drank. The liquor was heady, exhilarating, with a faintly brackish flavor.

And abruptly I knew why the pain-racked, ruined face of my companion had seemed familiar; I had seen it often among the portraits of my ancestors, the frowning, disfigured visage of the founder of the House of Kralitz that glared down from the gloom of the great hall. In that fierce white light of revelation I knew my companions for what they were; I recognized them, one by one, remembering their canvas counterparts. But there was a change! Like an impalpable veil, the stamp of ineradicable evil lay on the tortured faces of my hosts, strangely altering their features, so that I could not always be sure I recognized them. One pale, sardonic face reminded me of my father, but I could not be sure, so monstrously altered was its expression.

I was dining with my ancestors-the House of Kralitz!

My cup was still held high, and I drained it, for somehow the grim revelation was not entirely unexpected. A strange glow thrilled through my veins, and I laughed aloud for the evil delight that was in me. The others laughed too, a deep-throated merriment like the barking of wolves-tortured laughter from men stretched on the rack, mad laughter in hell! And all through the hazy cavern came the clamor of the devil's brood! Great figures that towered many spans high rocked with thundering glee, and the flying things tittered slyly overhead. And out over the vast expanse swept the wave of frightful mirth, until the half-seen things in the black waters sent out bellows that tore at my eardrums, and the unseen roof far overhead sent back roaring echoes of the clamor.

And I laughed with them, laughed insanely, until I dropped exhausted into my seat and watched the scarred man at the other end of the table as he spoke.

"You are worthy to be of our company, and worthy to eat at the same board. We have pledged each other, and you are one of us; we shall eat together."

And we fell to, tearing like hungry beasts at the succulent white meat in the jeweled trenchers. Strange monsters served us, and at a chill touch on my arm I turned to find a dreadful crimson thing, like a skinned child, refilling my goblet. Strange, strange and utterly blasphemous was our feast. We shouted and laughed and fed there in the hazy light, while all around us thundered the evil horde. There was hell beneath Castle Kralitz, and it held high carnival this night.

* * * * *

Presently we sang a fierce drinking-song, swinging the deep cups back and forth in rhythm with our shouted chant. It was an archaic song, but the obsolete words were no handicap, for I mouthed them as though they had been learned at my mother's knee. And at the thought of my mother a trembling and a weakness ran through me abruptly, but I banished it with a draft of the heady liquor.

Long, long we shouted and sang and caroused there in the great cavern, and after a time we arose together and trooped to where a narrow, high-arched bridge spanned the tenebrous waters of the lake. But I may not speak of what was at the other end of the bridge, nor of the unnamable things that I saw-and did! I learned of the fungoid, inhuman beings that dwell on far cold Yuggoth, of the cyclopean shapes that attend unsleeping Cthulhu in his submarine city, of the strange pleasures that the followers of leprous, subterranean Yog-Sothoth may possess, and I learned, too, of the unbelievable manner in which Iod, the Source, is worshipped beyond the outer galaxies. I plumbed the blackest pits of hell and came back-laughing. I was one with the rest of those dark warders, and I joined them in the saturnalia of horror until the scarred man spoke to us again.

"Our time grows short," he said, his scarred and bearded white face like a gargoyle's in the half-light. "We must depart soon. But you are a true Kralitz, Franz, and we shall meet again, and feast again, and make merry for longer than you think. One last pledge!"

I gave it to him. "To the House of Kralitz! May it never fall!"

And with an exultant shout we drained the pungent dregs of the liquor.

Then a strange lassitude fell upon me. With the others I turned my back on the cavern and the shapes that pranced and bellowed and crawled there, and I went up through the carved stone portal. We filed up the stairs, up and up, endlessly, until at last we emerged through the gaping hole in the stone flags and proceeded, a dark, silent company, back through those interminable corridors. The surroundings began to grow strangely familiar, and suddenly I recognized them.

We were in the great burial vaults below the castle, where the Barons Kralitz were ceremoniously entombed. Each Baron had been placed in his stone casket in his separate chamber, and each chamber lay, like beads on a necklace, adjacent to the next, so that we proceeded from the farthermost tombs of the early Barons Kralitz toward the unoccupied vaults. By immemorial custom, each tomb lay bare, an empty mausoleum, until the time had come for its use, when the great stone coffin, with the memorial inscription carved upon it, would be carried to its place. It was fitting, indeed, for the secret of Kralitz to be hidden here.

Abruptly I realized that I was alone, save for the bearded man with the disfiguring scar. The others had vanished, and, deep in my thoughts, I had not missed them. My companion stretched out his black-swathed arm and halted my progress, and I turned to him questioningly. He said in his sonorous voice, "I must leave you now. I must go back to my own place." And he pointed to the way whence we had come.

I nodded, for I had already recognized my companions for what they were. I knew that each Baron Kralitz had been laid in his tomb, only to arise as a monstrous thing neither dead nor alive, to descend into the cavern below and take part in the evil saturnalia. I realized, too, that with the approach of dawn they had returned to their stone coffins, to lie in a death-like trance until the setting sun should bring brief liberation. My own occult studies had enabled me to recognize these dreadful manifestations.

I bowed to my companion and would have proceeded on my way to the upper parts of the castle, but he barred my path. He shook his head slowly, his scar hideous in the phosphorescent gloom.

I said, "May I not go yet?"

He stared at me with tortured, smoldering eyes that had looked into hell itself, and he pointed to what lay beside me, and in a flash of nightmare realization I knew the secret of the curse of Kralitz. There came to me the knowledge that made my brain a frightful thing in which shapes of darkness would ever swirl and scream; the dreadful comprehension of *when* each Baron Kralitz was initiated into the brotherhood of blood. I knew —*I knew* —that no coffin had ever been placed unoccupied in the tombs, and I read upon the stone sarcophagus at my feet the inscription that made my doom known to me —*my own name, "Franz, twenty-first Baron Kralitz."*

"No! No!" he babbled, "not that!"

Chameleon Man

He was a changeable sort of fellow-and on occasions resembled a piecemeal zombie assembled by someone entirely ignorant of anatomy!

Tim Vanderhof wavered. He stood ten feet from a glass-paneled door, his apprehensive gaze riveted upon it, and swayed back and forth like a willow. Or, perhaps, an aspen. He wasn't sure. Yes, it was an aspen—a quaking aspen. His ears seemed to twitch gently as he listened to the low rumble of voices from the inner office of S. Horton Walker, president of The Svelte Shop, Fifth Avenue's snootiest establishment for supplying exclusive models of dresses, lingerie, and what-not.

Let us examine Mr. Vanderhof. He did not, at the moment, look like a man who, within a very short time, was going to turn into what amounted to something rather like a chameleon. Nevertheless, mentally and spiritually, Tim Vanderhof was a mere mass of quivering protoplasm, and no great wonder, after the interview he had just had. He wasn't bad looking, though slightly pallid. His features were regular, his face a bit chubby, and his eyes held the expression of a startled fawn. They were brown, like his hair, and he had a pug nose.

He shivered slightly as the glass-paneled door opened. A Back appeared. Under it were two short, slightly bowed legs, and it was surmounted by a scarlet billiard-ball of a head. There was no neck. The Bade was draped in tweeds, and a strong smell of tobacco, brandy, and horses emanated from it.

The Back extended a large, capable hand, clenched it into a fist, and shook it warningly at someone inside the office.

"Gad, sir!" a deep voice boomed, "Gad! This is the last straw! Mrs. Quester will be furious. And I warn you, Walker, that I shall be furious too. I have stood enough of your trifling. Twice already you promised exclusive models of a dress for my wife, and then failed to deliver."

"But—" said a Voice.

"*Silence!*" bellowed the Back, and the Voice was cowed. "You have promised Model Forty-Three to Mrs. Quester. If you dare to exhibit it at your fashion show this afternoon, I shall call upon you with a riding-whip. I shall be here after the show, and you will have the dress ready for me to take to Mrs. Quester. You have had enough time to make alterations. Gad, sir-in Burma I have had men broken—*utterly* broken-for less than this."

The Voice, with a faint spark of antagonism, rallied. It said, "But."

"But me no buts, damn your eyes! This isn't Burma, but you will find that Colonel Quester still knows how to use his fists-you *tradesman!* I shall be back this afternoon, and —*brrrrmph!*"

"Yes, Colonel," the Voice assented weakly, and the Back turned, revealing to the watching Vanderhof a round, crimson face with a bristling, iron-gray mustache, and beetling brows from beneath which lightning crackled menacingly. Brrmphing, Colonel Quester moved like a mastodon past the quaking Vanderhof and vanished through a door that seemed to open coweringly of its own accord at the man's advance. Vanderhof immediately turned and started to tiptoe away.

The Voice detected the sound of his departure. "Vanderhof!" it screamed. "Come here!"

Thus summoned, the unfortunate official halted, retraced his steps, and entered the inner sanctum. There he paused like a hypnotized rabbit, watching the Voice, who was also known as S. Horton Walker, president of The Svelte Shop.

A hard man, S. Horton Walker. As a child. he had pulled the wings off butterflies, and maturity had not improved him. He looked like a shaved ape, with a bristling crop of blue-black hair and a gleaming, vicious eye that was now engaged in skinning Vanderhof.

"UIp," the later remarked, in a conciliatory tone.

"Don't give me that," Walker growled, crouching behind his desk like the gorilla he resembled. "I told you to keep that so-and-so out of my office. Well?"

"I said you were out," Vanderhof explained. "I—I—"

"You-you—" Walker mocked, pointing a stubby sausage of a finger. "Bah! And, again, bah! What the hell are you, a man or a jellyfish?"

"A man," Vanderhof said hopefully.

Walker's grunt was profoundly skeptical. "You're a weakfish. A non-entity. By God, when I was your age I had twenty-nine men under me. By sheer force of personality I made myself what I am today. And I like men with drive-push-get-up-and-go."

Vanderhof, seeing an opportunity of escape, began to get-up-and-go, but relapsed at Walker's furious yelp. "Why, do you realize that Colonel Quester would have punched me in the eye if I hadn't impressed him with my personality? He's an outrageous person."

"You did promise those exclusive models to his wife though."

"We get a better price elsewhere," Walker said, and pondered. "But Model Forty-Three will be ready for him when he calls this afternoon. A dangerous man, the colonel. Where was I? Oh, yes. "You're a fool, Vanderhof."

Vanderhof nodded and looked like a fool. Walker groaned in exasperation. "Haven't you any personality at all? No, you haven't. You're a—a—a chameleon, that's what. I've noticed that before. When you're talking to a ditch-digger, you act like one yourself. When you're talking to a banker, you turn into a banker. You're a *mirror*, that's what!"

It was unfortunate that Vanderhof did not leave at that moment. After his interview with the excitable Colonel Quester, he was mere protoplasm, and somewhat too receptive to suggestion. It was, of course, true, that Vanderhof had little character of his own. He had lost it, after years of associating with the virulent Walker. He was a complete yes-man, and needed only a catalyst to complete a certain chemical reaction that was already taking place.

"*You're a chameleon*," Walker said, with emphasis, and his eyes bored into Vanderhof's.

It was at that precise moment that Mr. Tim Vanderhof turned into a chameleon.

Not physically, of course. The metamorphosis was far more subtle. Adept for years at assuming the traits of others, Vanderhof was rather shockingly receptive. Though all he did was to sit down in a chair opposite his boss.

Walker stared, frowned, and hesitated.

Vanderhof stared, frowned, and didn't say anything.

Walker lifted a large hand and pointed accusingly.

Vanderhof lifted a smaller hand and also pointed accusingly.

Walker flushed. So did Vanderhof.

The president of The Svelte Shop rose like a behemoth from his chair and growled, "Are you mocking me?"

Then he stopped, amazed, because Vanderhof had risen and said exactly the same thing.

"You-you-you—" Walker's face was purple. Vanderhof guessed what was coming. With a mighty effort he asserted what little remained of his will-power.

"D-don't go on!" he pleaded frantically. "P-please—"

"You chameleon!" S. Horton Walker thundered.

"*You chameleon!*" Vanderhof thundered.

Such bare-faced, impudent mockery was unendurable. Walker quivered in every muscle. "You're fired!" he said. "What's that? What did you say? What do you mean, I'm fired? Stop imitating me, you stupid clown. Don't call me a stupid clown! *Nrrgh!*"

"—nrrgh!" Vanderhof finished, not quite realizing what was happening to him. Walker sat down weakly. He was shaken a little, but his natural malignancy was still undimmed. A natural snake, S. Horton Walker.

"I—"

"I—" said Vanderhof.

Walker bellowed, *"Shut up!"* And, so strong was his will, for the moment Vanderhof remained perfectly quiet.

"Are you going to get out?" he asked at length, in a low, deadly voice. "Damn it, stop mocking me! I'll have you thrown out! *What?* Have me thrown out of my own office?"

Goaded to insensate fury by the fact that Vanderhof was repeating perfectly everything he said and did-and, curiously enough, at exactly the same time he said and did it-Walker stuck out his thumb to press a button on the desk. It collided with Vanderhof's thumb.

Walker sat back, palpitating, a mute Vesuvius. Obviously Vanderhof had gone mad. And yet —

"I wish you'd go and drown yourself," said the president, meaning every word. He was somewhat astonished when Tim Vanderhof quietly arose and left the office. He would have been even more surprised had he seen Vanderhof walk down 42nd Street to Times Square, and then board the Brighton Beach subway train bound for Coney Island. Somehow, it is doubtful whether Walker would have regretted the incident or recalled his words. He was evil to the core, and a hard man, as has been mentioned previously. He turned back to his preparations for the exclusive fashion show that afternoon, while the metamorphosed Tim Vanderhof hurried off to go and drown himself.

Now Tim was really a nice guy. He shot a fair game of golf, had once made ten straight passes while shooting craps at a stag party, and was kind to dogs, blind men, and small children. He explained the latter eccentricity by stating that he had once been a small child himself, which was no doubt true enough. Under other circumstances, Mr. Vanderhof might have achieved a genuine personality of his own, but he had the misfortune always to be associated with rats tike Walker. Self-riadc men invariably contend that they had to fight their way through obstacles, so they create new obstacles for those under them, probably with the best intentions in the world. The fact remains that Walker had provided the ultimate catalyst for Tim Vanderhof, who got off the subway at Coney Island-it had now, by some strange metamorphosis, been transformed into an elevated-and wandered along the boardwalk, peering contemplatively at the ocean.

It was large, gray, and wet. A great deal of H_2O, to put it scientifically. Vanderhof s mind was dulled; he found it difficult to think clearly, and he kept hearing Walker's command over and over again.

" —go and drown yourself. Go and drown yourself."

The sky was cloudy. It had been a hot day, one of those Turkish bath affairs which make Manhattan, in the summer, a suburb of hell, and so there were vast quantities of people at Coney. Large bulging women lumbered about shepherding brats, who fed voraciously on ice-cream, pickles, hokey-pokey, hot dogs, and similar juicy tidbits. Brawny young men and flimsy girls, hot and perspiring, tried to gulp down air quite as humid as in the city. Meanwhile, the Atlantic Ocean beckoned to Tim Vanderhof.

His eyes were glazed as he made a beeline for the nearest pier. In the back of his mind a little remnant of sanity shrieked warning, but Vanderhof could not obey. Stripped of the last remnant of personality and will-power, he walked on....

" —go and drown yourself. Go and drown yourself."

Vanderhof made a mighty effort to break the spell, but it was useless. He walked on, his gaze riveted on the greasy slate-colored water at the end of the pier. Not a man, woman, or child among the crowd noticed him. He tried to call for help, but no sound came from his lips.

People were running. Rain began to splash down, first in droplets, then in ever-increasing torrents. The gray clouds were fulfilling their promise. People ran, with newspapers over their heads, to the nearest shelter.

Wavering on the edge of the pier, Vanderhof felt something pull him back. Magnetically he was made to retreat a few staggering steps, He turned. He started to walk back along the wharf, then he was running with the rest of the crowd. No longer did he hear Walker's voice demanding suicide. In its place was an urgent whisper that said:

"Run! *Run!"*

Hundreds of men, women, and children were rushing to shelter. The effect of this mass he-gira was too much for the human chameleon. A wave seemed to bear him along with the others. Vainly he tried to struggle against the impulse. No use, of course. Rain splashed in his face.

It was like running in a dream, without conscious volition. Lines of force seemed to drag him onward. Off the pier. On the boardwalk, and along it, in the midst of the crowd. As various members of the mob dived for shelter, poor Vanderhof was tossed about like a leaf in a gale. A group leaped into a hot-dog stand, and Vanderhof veered after them. Then a larger group came past, and he skittered in their wake, utterly helpless.

They entered Luna Park, and he perforce followed.

Somehow he was caught in the eddy, and found himself, limp and perspiring, in a penny arcade, almost deserted. A semblance of sanity came back to him. Gasping and drenched to the skin, Vanderhof cowered behind a "grind-box" labeled "Paris Night-For Men Only," and wondered what in hell was happening to him.

He tried to think. What had Walker said? A human chameleon. It seemed to have come true. Adept for years at assuming the traits of others, the ultimate transformation had taken place, ever he looked at anyone now, he assumed the traits of that person.

It was really far worse, only Vanderhof didn't realize it quite yet.

Logically, the only solution was to stay away from people. A man without personality is bound to reflect the personality of others. Vanderhof peeped out, looking glumly at a rotund little man with white whiskers who was standing at the entrance to the arcade, staring virtuously at nothing. A pleasant little man, he thought. He probably had not a worry in the world. Vanderhof wished he were that man.

He was startled by the sound of footsteps, and even more startled when a veritable giantess of a woman smacked him over the head with her umbrella. The unfortunate Vanderhof reeled, seeing stars. He gasped, "W-w-wha —"

"Worm!" the Amazon boomed. "I told you not to enter this-this *peep-show!*" Her voice quivered with menace. Utterly at a loss, Vanderhof raised his hand to his stinging head, but it was entrapped halfway in what seemed to be a maze of dangling spaghetti. He investigated. It was a set of white whiskers, exactly like the man at whom he had been looking-only the whiskers were on Vanderhof's face!

The giantess had turned momentarily to wither the arcade with a glance, and Vanderhof caught sight of himself in a nearby mirror. It did not, however, much resemble Tim Vanderhof. What he saw was a rotund little man with white whiskers.

With an astonished shriek Vanderhof turned back to his normal self. The apparition in the mirror resumed its usual and familiar semblance. It was again Tim Vanderhof.

"Oh, my God," the man murmured faintly. "I'm dreaming."

"What?" The Amazon turned, her umbrella raised. Then her eyes dilated. How the devil had her husband managed to get out of sight so suddenly, leaving an utter stranger in place of himself? She didn't know. She stared balefully at Vanderhof, who shrank back, his eyes on the umbrella.

Just then the giantess caught sight of the fat little man at the arcade's entrance. She turned, lumbering away. This time she disdained the use of the umbrella. Going, apparently, on a variation of the principle that fingers were made before forks, she lifted a ham-like hand and smote the, fat little man athwart the ear. The beard rippled like a white banner as the wretched creature was hurled out into the rain.

He raised himself from the mud and dazedly contemplated his wife. She had never before struck him without good cause-what she considered good cause, anyway. If she was going to beat him on sudden, mad impulses, the future would be dark indeed, thought the fat little man.

He rose and ran rapidly away.

The giantess followed, crying threats.

Tim Vanderhof shuddered convulsively. He was going insane. Or else.... No, it was too ghastly. He couldn't be a jellyfish as well as a chameleon. He might, perhaps, assume the traits of somebody else, but he *couldn't* acquire their actual physical appearance as well!

"No," Vanderhof said urgently. "Please —*no!*"

Yet it was profoundly and disturbingly logical. He had looked at the fat little man, and had become the fat little man, white whiskers and all. The shock of seeing himself in the mirror had caused him to return to a more normal appearance. What would be the ultimate result? Would Tim Vanderhof fade into a shadow —a mere thing? Yipe.

Such was the cry that burst from Vanderhof's dry throat at the very prospect. He couldn't go about the world turning into everybody he met. And yet-chameleons did it, in so far as pigmentation went. A specialized animal like a man might go even further. The powers of the mind and the will were unplumbed. Vanderhof knew that, from much perusal of Sunday supplements and science-fiction magazines. Recalling stories he had read by such authors as H. G. Wells, Jules Verne, and Henry Kuttner, he groaned as he realized that the heroes of such tales usually met a sticky end.

"Oh, no!" Vanderhof whispered involuntarily. "I don't want to die. I'm too young to die."

Footsteps clumped into the arcade. Hurriedly Vanderhof whirled, burying his face in the nearest slot-machine, which featured a presumably authentic reel telling how native women were kidnapped by gorillas in the Congo. It was neither natural shyness nor a genuine interest in anthropology which caused Vanderhof's sudden retreat. He feared to face anyone, believing, logically enough, that he might turn into that person.

He dropped a penny in the slot and whirled the crank, scarcely seeing the faded cards that flickered into view and out again inside the machine. A gorilla was engaged in wandering through its native jungle.

Someone behind Vanderhof began to laugh maniacally. His cries rose into shrill screams.

There were answering, inquiring shouts. Feet thudded. Someone called, "What's the matter there."

"A monkey!" came the hysterical response. "There's a gorilla looking at dirty pictures! I've got the jumping jitters again!"

Vanderhof hurriedly turned to face a tall, skinny man with a horselike face and bloodshot eyes. He carried a cane and apparently a large cargo of Scotch.

"It's coming after me!" the man screeched, retreating. "First snakes, and now this. Ah-h, those awful glaring eyes!"

"Sh-h!" said Vanderhof, lifting a placating hand. The drunk shivered in every limb.

"It hisses like a snake!" he cried, and thrust out the cane like a fencer. Its metal tip caught Vanderhof in the middle, and he doubled up, breathless and gasping. And, simultaneously, he saw himself in a mirror.

It didn't look like Tim Vanderhof. It was wearing Tim Vanderhof's clothes, but it was, un-questionably a gorilla-the kind that kidnap native women in the Congo. The sound of footsteps grew louder. The new arrivals were almost at the arcade.

Vanderhof put forth a mighty effort of will, inadvertently baring his fangs. The drunk emitted a short, sharp cry and covered his eyes. But Vanderhof ignored him. He was glaring, wildly, at the mirror.

And, suddenly, the gorilla was gone. Vanderhof was himself again.

Tenderly rubbing his stomach, Vanderhof straightened to meet the red-rimmed gaze of the horse-faced man.

"Where is it?" the latter babbled. "Where did it go?"

"Where did what go?" Vanderhof asked coldly, still maintaining the mental effort that enabled him to keep his rightful form.

"The gorilla —" There was a pause as people poured into the arcade, asking questions. There was confusion and tumult. And shouting. This died, eventually, as Vanderhof indicated the horse-faced man and explained that he was drunk.

"I'm not that drunk," was the surly response. "Snakes, yes. But not gorillas. Where is it? I know." The man's glazed eyes brightened. "You hid it!"

"You're drunk," Vanderhof said.

"Yeah? For two cents I'd punch your face in. Gr-r!" His confusion crystallized into belligerency, the drunk rolled forward, waving the cane. Vanderhof fled —

It was a hard life, he thought dismally, as he slunk through Luna Park, carefully avoiding crowds. The rain had stopped now, but people were still wary. This was all to the good. Vanderhof could, he found, retain his normal shape by putting forth a strong mental effort, but this could not be kept up for long. Already he felt weak.

Yet, at the back of his mind, a queer, perverse excitement was slowly, imperceptibly growing. In a way, it was rather fun. Imagine being able to turn yourself into a gorilla! Everybody was afraid of gorillas!

People shot them, too, Vanderhof recalled, and shut his eyes. He wavered, hearing faintly the tones of a hoarse, rasping voice that plucked at his nerves. It was like-like-what?"

Like Walker's voice. Urgent-commanding. Demanding that he do something —

He opened his eyes and found himself before a side-show. The barker stood above him on a box, derby tilted back, checkered suit, garish, thrusting out a commanding finger.

"C'mon, folks! Here it is, greatest sideshow on Earth! Tiniest dwarf ever born of woman, tallest giant since Creation, all the wonders of the Universe gathered here for your inspection. Step inside! You, there-only a dime. Step right forward, mister! The girl will take your dime!"

"No!" Vanderhof squeaked faintly, and tried to retreat. Instead, he found himself walking forward.

"Right this way, mister! Pay your dime! *R-r-right* in here! Step inside —"

Vanderhof found a dime and paid the admission charge. He didn't want to go into the sideshow. He had a singularly horrid idea of what might happen there. But the barker's will-power was too strong for him,, and he could no longer exert the mental effort that partially insulated him from danger. He was exhausted.

"I'm a jellyfish," poor Vanderhof "mourned as he entered the show. "That's what I am. Walker was right. Oh, damn!" he ended futilely, tears of frustrated rage in his eyes. "I wish this would stop!"

But wishing didn't do any good. The chameleon man found himself in the sideshow-surrounded by freaks!

He caught one glimpse of innumerable people-terrifying to him, under the circumstances-ranged around the big room, and then fled through a doorway on his right. It was definitely no time to face giants, dwarfs, dog-faced boys, or wild men from Sumatra. Vanderhof wanted only peace and quiet.

He got neither.

He found himself in a small anteroom containing a mirror and a dwarf. The latter whirled and snapped. "Didn't you see the sign over the door? This is private! I-huh?"

He stopped talking, and presently resumed. "Say, that's a clever trick. Are you one of the boys? A magician, huh?"

"Yeah," said the now dwarfish Mr. Vanderhof. "I d-do it with mirrors."

"Damn good," returned the little man, whose name was Bingo. "Wait a minute. I want Ajax to see this."

"Don't bother," Vanderhof started, but he was too late. Bingo whistled, and immediately the room was darkened by the shadow of Ajax, who was seven feet nine inches tall, and would have had no need for snowshoes.

Vanderhof shut his eyes. He tried to assert his will-power, or what little remained of it, and was rewarded with pleased noises from giant and dwarf. "Clever!" said the latter. "Did you see that? He was little a minute ago. Now he isn't."

"That's right," the giant rumbled. "He looked like you, too, Bingo. Did you notice? Who are you, Mister?'"

"I wish I knew," Vanderhof gasped, feeling lost and helpless. He dared not open his eyes. He was again in his normal semblance, but the very sight of either Ajax or Bingo might cause another metamorphosis.

"You!" a new voice broke in-one familiar to Vanderhof as that of the drunk in the arcade. "I been looking for you. I want to punch you in the snoot."

Vanderhof, feeling set-upon, almost had a mad impulse to sock the drunk, but habit prevailed. He took refuge in flight, or tried to. Unfortunately, he ran into the mirror, bumped his nose, and turned, opening his eyes.

He saw Ajax and Bingo.

The drunk lunged forward, lifting his cane. Then he halted, and a scream of stark terror burst from his throat.

"*Yaaaah!*" he shrieked. Apparently considering this an insufficient comment, he threw up his hands and added, "Waaaah!"

He fled, leaving a memento in the form of his cane, which he flung at Vanderhof with unerring aim. Nose and cane collided.

Ajax and Bingo whistled in chorus: 'Wow!" said the latter. "Didja see that? Mister, you're good! You almost scared me."

Vanderhof, tears of pain in his eyes, turned to the mirror. "Yeah," he said in a shaky voice. "You may not believe it, but I'm scaring myself. Am I crazy, or do I look like both of you?"

"Well," the dwarf said judiciously, "the top part of you looks like me, but the bottom half looks like Ajax. *I* don't see how you do it. You must be on the big time."

Vanderhof was silent, considering the impossible reflection in the mirror. From the waist up he was Bingo, the dwarf. His lower extremities were those of a giant. The result was harrowing in the extreme. It was like putting a chameleon on Scotch plaid.

With a mighty effort he resumed his normal appearance. There were cries of amazement and appreciation from his companions. Leaving them to their simple pleasures, Vanderhof walked unsteadily back into the main show. He was bound for fresh air-lots of it. And peace.

Chameleons, however, do not lead peaceful lives, contrary to the opinions of some. The unexpected is always happening.

As Vanderhof crossed the big room, he was trying to understand what had happened. He had assumed the outward appearance of two people at the same time-abnormal people at that. Things were getting worse. Ajax and Bingo. Bingo and Ajax. Giant and —

Whup! Vanderhof had entered another room, over the doorway of which was a sign reading, "Magic Mirrors," and paused, facing the only normal mirror in the place. He was looking at the same conglomeration of dwarf and giant that he had viewed before.

Good Lord! Could he change his shape by merely —*thinking?* The thought was appalling, yet it possessed a curious, perverse fascination for Vanderhof. Standing perfectly motionless, he concentrated on his own normal self.

And there was the reflection of Tim Vanderhof facing him!

That, at least, was a relief. But, feeling slightly safer now, Vanderhof didn't stop. He wanted to make sure. He thought of the side-show barker outside, and visualized him mentally. Derby hat, cigar, checkered suit.

The reflection in the glass showed the barker, though there was neither derby, cigar, nor checkered suit. Apparently only Vanderhof himself could change. His clothing remained un-altered. That was natural enough.

He returned to his normal self.

"You!" said a familiar voice. "I been looking for you! None of your tricks, now! I wanna punch your nose."

"Oh, my goodness!" Vanderhof said, turning. "You again!"

"Yeah!" said the drunk belligerently. "Wanna make something out of it?" He lifted the cane and advanced. Vanderhof, perforce, retreated into the room of Magic Mirrors. He found liimself being backed into a corner, his fascinated gaze riveted on the cane. Its metal tip looked extremely hard. The drunk had recovered it, or else acquired a new one. In any case, it seemed to be a dangerous weapon.

The horsey face bore a malignant expression. "I'm gonna smash you," it said, and thrust itself forward. Vanderhof backed away, feeling the cold surface of a mirror at his back. He was trapped. The room was empty. No use to call for help. The din from the next room, where a band was loudly playing, would drown any but the loudest shrieks.

Abruptly Vanderhof felt irritation. His stomach was still sore from the cane's tip, and his nose, too, was aching. He said, "Go away."

"No," the drunk growled. "I'm gonna smash you."

Sudden, violent rage boiled up in Vanderhof. He thought of Ajax and Bingo. If they were there, they'd help him. But —

Vanderhof thought diligently, visualizing giant and dwarf. From the startled look that came over the drunk, he realized that the metamorphosis had once again taken place.

He stepped forward, warily at first, and the horse-faced man retreated.

At that precise moment Vanderhof caught sight of himself in one of the mirrors that lined the place. The change was not quite the same as before. This time, from the waist down, Vanderhof was Bingo, the dwarf. His upper portion resembled Ajax the giant.

Nor was that the worst. The mirror that reflected the insane image was no normal one. It was a distorting mirror, designed to cause laughter by warping and twisting images. Concave, it reflected Vanderhof not only as a half-giant, half-dwarf, but as a swooping arc — a being bent like a bow, such as had never before existed on Earth.

The drunk shrieked. "No, no!" he babbled. "Not that!"

Vanderhof realized that he had taken on the attributes of the distorted image. He glanced at the cowering horse-faced man, and felt a warm glow of triumph.

It faded as he was punched in the stomach by the cane.

Vanderhof got mad. He said, with slow emphasis, "Okay. You asked for it. Now you're going to —*get it!*"

The other showed his teeth.

Vanderhof looked at the nearest mirror. The result was shocking, but did not quite satisfy him. He looked at another, and then another, after that turning to confront his enemy.

Not even Samson could have faced the chaotic Vanderhof without screaming then. He looked like a piecemeal zombie assembled by someone with no knowledge of anatomy. One leg was six feet longer than the other. He had five arms. His chest was like a balloon, and his waist measured perhaps three inches around.

His head resembled a fried egg that had broken in the pan. The mouth was, oddly enough, in the forehead, and there was a tasty assortment of eyes scattered around them, all of these glaring furiously. He towered to the ceiling, and the horse-faced man, giving up all thought of hostility, skittered away like a rabbit.

"Go 'way!" he babbled. "Don't touch me! You're not human, that's what you ain't!"

"You don't get out of it that easily," Vanderhof snapped, barring the door with a fifteen-foot arm. "What do you think I am, anyhow?"

"The devil himself," said the drunk, with a flash of sudden insight. "*Awrrrgh!* Don't do that!"

"I'll do it again," Vanderhof announced, and a scream of pain from the drunk bore testimony to the fact that he had done it again. "Thus."

The wild and impassioned shrieks of the horse-faced man bore fruit. Vanderhof heard faint cries from behind him. He turned to see faces peering in through the door.

They went white and drew back. Someone cried, "A freak! He's gone mad!"

"He's murdering me!" the drunk announced. "Help!"

Heartened by reinforcements, he made the mistake of prodding Vanderhof from the rear with his cane. At this all semblance of sanity departed from Tim Vanderhof. Completely forgetting everything else, he bent all his energies to the task of reducing the horse-faced man to a state of babbling idiocy.

"Give me that cane!" he grated.

"So you can ram it down my throat?" came the prescient reply. "I won't."

At this Vanderhof looked in a mirror, sprouted another arm, grew two feet, and advanced toward his opponent. He got the cane and broke it into six pieces. One in each hand, he commenced to tattoo a rhythm on the drunk.

This wasn't quite satisfactory, so he gave it up, and concentrated on scaring the wretched man to death. Never was any revenge more horrifying or complete. Vanderhof felt a random sense of warning; it might be wiser, safer, to leave now, before more trouble arrived. But-what the hell!

He grinned, and the horse-faced man bellowed in anguish. "He's going to eat me!" he cried. "Don't let him eat me!"

"There they are," someone observed. "In there, Sergeant. It's a freak. Quite mad."

"It's a freak, all right," said a gruff voice. "But I'm thinking that I'm the looney one. Will you look at the horrid thing!"

"I've been looking at it for ten minutes," said the other voice. "Ever since I turned in the alarm. You've got your squad with you. Arrest him before he kills that man."

Vanderhof turned. The doorway held a burly, grizzled oldster in police uniform, and behind him a group of plainclothes men, their profession easily established by a glance at their feet. There were guns.

He was sent staggering. The horsefaced man had made a break for freedom. Vanderhof, boiling with rage, plunged in pursuit. There was chaos on the threshold; then Vanderhof was past, and racing after his victim.

A bullet whistled past his ear.

Oh-oh! This altered matters. Vanderhof, hidden momentarily behind the bandstand, paused, looking around. He saw no one —the horse-faced man had vanished-but heard voices.

"He went behind there-get him-guns ready, men!"

Vanderhof thought hard. He visualized the drunk. And, instantly, he assumed the appearance of the drunk.

He ran out from behind the bandstand, almost colliding with the sergeant and a plainclothes man with him.

"Hey —"

"He went that way!" Vanderhof cried. "After him! Don't let him get away!"

Without waiting for an answer, he ran for the exit. There was startled silence, and then the sergeant and his crew raced in pursuit.

Vanderhof leaped out into the open air, flattened himself against the wall of the building, and concentrated on the face of the plainclothes man who had accompanied the sergeant. And, of course, the inevitable happened.

The sergeant appeared. He cast a swift glance at Vanderhof.

"Where is he, Clancy?" he bellowed. "Which way did he go?"

"There!" said the pseudo-Clancy, and pointed. He was borne away in a mob of detectives who gushed out of the exit. All of them were busily searching for a freak with six arms and an impossible head —a freak who no longer existed!

Ten minutes later Vanderhof, in his normal guise, was on the train bound back for Manhattan. It had been easy to drift away from the detectives, who naturally suspected nothing. And, after that, Vanderhof wanted only to get away from Coney Island. His nerves were in bad shape. He needed a rest.

So, illogically enough, he went back to New York.

He was still angry about the horse-faced man. He would have dearly loved to have taken another poke at the guy. But the police had interrupted. Vanderhof's resentment wandered, and finally focused on a man with bristling blue-black hair and a vicious gleam in his eyes. The guy looked uncommonly like S. Horton Walker, president of The Svelte Shop.

Walker-nuts to Walker, Vanderhof thought. "Fire me, will he?" the chameleon man brooded. "Just on account of Colonel Quester! Tchah!" The fashion show would be going on soon, he remembered. And, simultaneously with the thought, Vanderhof grinned.

A singularly malicious and unpleasant grin....

"Fire me, will he?" he asked rhetorically, turning into Ajax for a brief moment. "I'll fix him!"

While making his way toward the Fifth Avenue store, he pondered. He was achieving some sort of mastery over his chameleon-like changes. If he visualized a person, he could become that person-though his clothing never altered. And, with an effort of will, he could resume his normal form. Good enough. What now?

The fashion show was in full swing when Vanderhof slipped quietly into The Svelte Shop, unobtrusively making his way behind the scenes. Dowagers and damsels in tons of jewelry were sitting about, feeding on canapes and *hors d'ouevres.* while all sorts and conditions of men waited uneasily upon their respective daughters, wives, and lady friends. Park Avenue had turned out in force for the initial showing of exclusive gowns by The Svelte Shop. Mannequins were gliding along the runways, and over all presided the figure of S. Horton Walker, resplendent in specially-tailored garments, and looking more than ever like a shaved ape.

"And Model Twelve?" a slightly decayed socialite inquired from above her tiers of chins. "The exclusive Model Twelve, Mr. Walker?"

"Soon," said Walker, rubbing his hands. "Very soon, Mrs. Smythe-Kennicott-Smythe."

Peering through drapes of wine-colored fabric, Vanderhof sucked in his lower lip. Model Twelve was already famous.

It was super-exclusive. Only one gown on this model had been created. And, when it showed, the bidding would be high-almost like an auction, though, of course, most genteel. Mrs. Smythe-Kennicott-Smythe would probably get it. She was the wealthiest woman in New York, and cream on the elite's upper crust, to put it mildly.

"Nuts to you, Mr. Walker," Vanderhof said silently, and fled. He made his way to the dressing-rooms, pausing at sight of Susan Vail; the shop's loveliest model. The girl nodded, smiled, and went on her way.

Vanderhof visualized her. Suddenly he was gone. A perfect duplicate of Susan Vail stood in the passage, looking rather odd in Tim Vandcrhof's garments.

"Now for Model Twelve. It was carefully stored away, but Vanderhof knew where to look. Tenderly, almost reverently, he drew it from its hiding-place, and held up the gown. It was a gorgeous creation-one that would transform any woman.

"Why, Susan," a soft voice said, "what are you doing in those clothes?"

Vanderhof turned hurriedly, to confront a small brown-haired model with wide eyes. "I —"

"And what's the matter with your voice? Got a cold?"

"No," said Vanderhof shrilly. "It-it's just a gag." Seizing Model Twelve, he fled into the nearest dressing-room.

A few minutes later he came out, wearing the gown. Since he looked exactly like Susan Vail, it wasn't at all unbecoming. But his plans weren't finished yet. He wanted to perform an experiment.

He entered a room replete with tall mirrors, reflecting him from various angles. And he concentrated. If he could become two men at once, surely he could transform himself into two or more Susan Vails.

The results were beyond all expectations. From every angle Susan Vails materialized. They appeared like rabbits out of a hat. And all of them wore Model Twelve.

Meanwhile, Walker was preening himself as he made the announcement for which everyone was waiting.

"And now, ladies and gentlemen, the event of the afternoon. At great expense, we have secured an ultra-exclusive model—a veritable symphony. There is only one like it in the world."

"How do we know that?" asked a skeptical man with sideburns.

Walker turned a hurt stare upon him. "The Svelte Shop stands ready to guarantee my statement. Our integrity has never been questioned. And now-Model Twelve!"

He flung out an arm toward the runway. The curtains shook convulsively. Through them appeared Susan Vail. A soft gasp went up from the women at sight of Model Twelve.

Then another gasp went up. Another Susan Vail had slipped through the curtains and was following in the track of the first. She, too, wore Model Twelve.

"Hey—" said the skeptical man with sideburns.

He stopped. A third Model Twelve was coming.

Then another. And another!

"My God!" the skeptical man gasped. "Quintuplets!"

Walker had turned a delicate shade of mauve. Cries of outraged fury went up from the audience. "Exclusive model," somebody snapped. "Hah!"

Meanwhile the army of Model Twelves was marching steadily through the curtains. The room was filled with them. Walker was clawing at his hair and making gurgling sounds. Mrs. Smythe-Kennicott-Smythe arose, waggled her chins haughtily, and departed.

"One might as well shop in the five-and-ten," she observed.

"It's sabotage! " Walker whispered faintly. "B-boring from within —"

His eyes brightened a trifle. Mrs. Smythe-Kennicott-Smythe had reconsidered. She wasn't leaving, after all. She was returning, her eyes very wide, and behind her was a large, bulky man with a mask on his face.

Other men arrived. Five of them. And they had guns, and were masked.

"This," said the leader, "is a stick-up. Squat, beetle-puss." He pushed Mrs. Smythe-Kennicott-Smythe into a chair. "And keep your trap shut. That goes for all of you." He waved a gleaming automatic. "Cover the exits, boys."

The boys obeyed. The guests sat, frozen with horror. One dowager attempted to swallow her diamonds, but was dissuaded. Walker gasped for air.

"This will ruin me!" he squawked. "My customers-my clients, I mean —"

"Shaddap," remarked the big man. "Or I'll let you have it. Don't anybody move. Frisk 'em, boys."

One of the boys produced a canvas bag and made the rounds, collecting whatever and money he could unearth. A pearl necklace, the existence of which had heretofore gone unsuspected, was revealed when Mrs. Smythe-Kennicott-Smythe was compelled to stare ceiling-ward.

"Hey!" said one of the boys. "What the hell-what —ulp!"

"Lcok!" he finished. "Jeez, boos-look!"

The big man looked. He, too, stared. Model Twelve was in action.

There were about twenty Susan Vails lined up on the runway. The last of them had stepped forward and-merged-with the one in front of her. This, Vanderhof had found, was the only way of consolidating his various images. He merely had to walk into himself.

The nineteenth Susan Vail merged with the eighteenth. And the eighteenth stepped forward —

Nobody else moved.

There was a stricken silence as the fifteenth Susan Vail became the fourteenth-and so on-the third became the second; there was only one Susan Vail now.

She hurried toward the exit.

But now the stasis broke. One of the thugs barred her path, lifting his gun menacingly.

Susan Vail-or Vanderhof-veered aside, toward an ante-room lined with mirrors. She ducked into it and slid die curtain in place after her.

The leader snapped, "Get her, Phil."

Phil said reluctantly, "There ain't no way for her to get outa there."

"I said —"

"Okay," Phil placated. "Just gimme time. That dame ain't normal."

He moved forward, gun lifted. His hand touched the curtain. Then he turned. "Boss, there ain't nothing in there but a lot of mirrors. What's the use —"

"You heard me!" the boss yelped.

"Okay," said Phil, and yanked the curtain aside.

Apparently there was another way out of the ante-room, for Susan Vail wasn't there any more. Instead, there were fifteen men, and they all looked exactly like Tim Vanderhof. Oddly enough, they all wore Model Twelve.

"*Yaah!*" said Phil shrilly, staggering back.

Two Tim Vanderhofs sprang upon him. One struck the gun from his hand, while the other planted a hard fist on Phil's jaw. The thug folded up limply.

One Vanderhof had pulled the curtain back into place, but Vanderhofs were emerging through it in twos, threes, and dozens. The room was suddenly flooded with Vanderhofs, all wearing Model Twelve. It was as though the ante-room had suddenly decided to give birth. It erupted Vanderhofs. It spewed them forth, and as fast as they emerged new ones followed. For there were many mirrors in that little room.

The element of surprise was in Vanderhof's favor. The crooks were struck dumb by this insane manifestation of men in evening gowns. Before they could recover, each one found himself borne down under a tangle of slugging, punching, kicking, homicidally-active Vanderhofs.

Mrs. Smythe-Kennicott-Smythe threw up her hands in hob horror. A Vanderhof paused to chuck her under the chins. "Keep your shirt on, babe," he advised. "I'll get your jewels back." The lady fainted.

Not all the Vanderhofs were engaged in taking care of the crooks. Twenty of them had mounted the runway and were delicately parading, showing off Model Twelve, which, to say the least, looked rather startling on Tim Vanderhofs masculine figure. A half-dozen more had surrounded the pallid, paralyzed Walker and were engaged in making horrific faces at him. Another group of Vanderhofs were holding an impromptu jam session in a corner, while still another had recaptured the canvas bag and was strewing its contents around the room, shouting, "Pig pig pig pig" in a hoarse voice. The clients were on hands and knees, scrambling after their stolen property.

It was a scene of utter chaos.

And Tim Vanderhof was-or were-having a glorious time. He hadn't enjoyed himself so much in years. He was doing a dozen different things, all at the same time, and the most delightful one of all dealt with the thugs, who by this time were trying only to escape from the veritable army that was assailing them.

Someone cried, "The police!"

That brought Vanderhof bade to sanity. He hurriedly knocked out the thugs-not a difficult task, since they were already nearly smothered by sheer weight of numbers-and then fled in a body, leaving confusion in his wake.

When the police arrived, they found six unconscious gangsters and a horde of socialites on hands and knees, squabbling over the division of their property. Walker was counting his fingers, with a vague air of skeptical disbelief. And there was no sign of a Vanderhof.

Indeed, there was only one Vanderhof by that time. The process of assimilation had again taken place, and the resultant single Vanderhof had removed Model Twelve-now torn into shreds-and resumed his own clothing. He didn't wait for events to happen, though. He took them into his own hands.

The elevator lifted him fifteen stories above Fifth Avenue, letting him out at the private office of Enoch Throckmorton, the actual owner of The Svelte Shop, as well as a number of other enterprises. Vanderhof had never seen Throckmorton; there were vague rumors of his existence on some Olympian height. Walker sometimes visited the man, and even dined with him on occasion. Now, leaving the elevator, Vanderhof thought of Walker, and visualized the man, blue-black hair, flashing eyes, and apish face.

"Good afternoon, Mr. Walker," said the receptionist. "Go right in."

Vanderhof nodded and opened a door, facing a glass-brick desk about a mile long. Behind it sat a shriveled little fellow who was chewing a cigar.

This was Enoch Throckmorton.

Or, better yet: This was —*Enoch Throckmorton!*

"Ha," said Throckmorton in a cracked voice, "sit down, Walker. I've just been getting a telephone call from downstairs. Quite a little fuss, eh?"

"Nothing much," Vanderhof shrugged, grinning to himself. Apparently his resemblance to Walker was so complete that even Throckmorton was deceived.

"Nothing much! Indeed! This man Vanderhof deserves recognition! He captured those bandits himself-we'd have had to make good on every cent stolen if he hadn't. I still don't know how he did it, but-he did it. That's the important thing."

"Well," Vanderhof said, "I've been intending to talk to you about Vanderhof for some time. He's the smartest man we have. Candidly, I think he deserves promotion."

"Very well. What have you in mind?"

"Manager. At a corresponding salary."

Throckmorton said slowly, "You know, of course, that the manager of The Svelte Shop is responsible only to me. You will have no authority over Vanderhof if—"

"I know my limitations," Vanderhof shrugged. "Vanderhof needs no discipline."

"Very well," said Throckmorton, pressing a button. "'Til attend to it immediately."

"Uh —" Vanderhof stood up. "By the way-if I should change my mind —"

Steel glinted in Throckmorton's beady eyes. "Indeed! You should have thought of that before. Do you, or do you not, recommend Vanderhof's promotion."

"I do."

"Then he's promoted. And the matter is now out of your hands-entirely!"

Vanderhof smiled and turned. He walked out on clouds. He did not even know that the elevator was taking him downstairs. Nuts to Walker....

So engrossed was he in day-dreams that he forgot to resume his normal appearance by the time he reached the general offices-which was, save for one person, deserted. This person wore tweeds, and now turned a round, crimson face and a bristling mustache on Vanderhof. It was Colonel Quester.

"Hah!" the colonel bellowed gently. "There you are! I see you've kept me waiting again."

"Uh —"

"Silence!" said Colonel Quester, and the ceiling shook. "I have come for Model Forty-three. Mrs. Quester's still furious, but the gown will placate her, I am sure. Is it ready? It had better be."

"Yes," said Vanderhof faintly. "I —I'll get it."

He fled. He got Model Forty-three. And, looking into a nearby mirror, he saw that he still exactly resembled S. Horton Walker.

Carrying the gown over his arm, on the way back he met one of the models. "Why, there you are, Mr. Walker," the girl said. "I thought you were in your office."

"I —uh-just stepped out for a minute."

So Walker was in his office! Vanderhof started to grin. He was beaming like a Cheshire cat when he entered the room where Colonel Quester waited, rumbling faintly like a miniature Vesuvius.

But the colonel softened at sight of the dress. "Ha!" he remarked. "A beauty! It is exclusive, you say?"

Vanderhof stepped back a pace. "The only one in existence," he remarked. "How do you like it, bottle-nose?"

There was a dead silence. Colonel Quester breathed through his nose. At last he asked, in a quiet voice, "What did you say?"

"Bottle-nose was the term," said Vanderhof happily. "Also, now that I think of it, you rather resemble a wart-hog."

"*Brrrmph!*" Quester rumbled warningly.

"*Brrrmph* to you," said Vanderhof. "You rhinocerous. So you want Model Forty-three, do you, fathead? Well, look."

He held up Model Forty-three, and with a strong tug ripped the dress from top to bottom. Quester turned magenta.

Vanderhof ripped the dress again.

Quester turned blue.

Vanderhof finished the job by ripping Model Forty-three into ribbons and throwing it into the colonel's face. Then he waited.

Colonel Quester was having difficulty in breathing. His mighty fists were clenched. "Wait," he promised. "Just wait till I control my blood-pressure. I'll break you for this —"

He took a step forward, and simultaneously Vanderhof dived for the inner office. He slipped through the door, held it shut behind him, and saw before him the blue-black thatch of S. Horton Walker, who was looking down at some papers on his desk.

Vanderhof asserted his will-power. Instantly he changed his shape.

Walker looked up. "Vanderhof?" he snapped. "I want to talk to you —"

"Just a minute. You have a caller."

"Wait!"

Vanderhof didn't wait. He stepped out of the office, carefully closing the door, and turned to confront Colonel Quester.

"Ah," he said. "What can I do for you, Colonel?"

"Get out of my way," said Quester, in a low, impassioned voice.

"With pleasure," Vanderhof smiled, stepping aside. "If you're looking for Mr. Walker, he's right inside."

To this the colonel made no answer. He entered the inner office, and Vanderhof gently shut the door after him. There was a brief silence.

It was broken by a dull thud, and a short, sharp cry, mingled with a bellow of triumph. Other noises followed.

"Model Forty-three, hey?" a hoarse voice boomed. "By Gad, sir, you'll eat it!"

"Ah?" Vanderhof murmured, walking away. "That lace collar should make a tasty mouthful."

He dusted his hands delicately. He was thinking that he had managed to acquire a personality of his own, and that his weird power of metamorphosis would gradually fade and vanish of its own accord. He was no longer a jellyfish —a chameleon.

He was the manager of The Svelte Shop. A choked gurgle of stark anguish came faintly from the distance.

Tim Vanderhof lifted his eyebrows. "Heigh-ho," he observed. "It's five o'clock. Another day."

Made in the USA
Monee, IL
27 August 2021